The Flaxborough Novels

'Watson's Flaxborough begins to take on the solidity of Bennett's Five Towns, with murder, murky past and much acidic comment added.'

H. R. F. KEATING

Lonelyheart 4122

Ah!

Right at the bottom of the column, it was. Something for which she had not dared to hope. Not in remote, prosperous, hard-headed Flaxborough.

A matrimonial bureau.

Well, what else could be meant by 'Handclasp House: Are you weary of the solitary path?'

Miss Teatime read the whole advertisement through carefully. Clients from all walks of life . . . introductions arranged . . . view to permanent association . . . countless instances of happiness . . . small initial fee . . . There was no doubt about it.

She took from her handbag a little lavender-coloured memorandum book. As she jotted down the address of Handclasp House, a smile spread over her face, illuminating charmingly its lineaments of good breeding.

Then she put the book away, folded the *Flaxborough Citizen* and resumed her contemplation of the waterside and the circling gulls.

The Flaxborough Novels

Whatever's Been Going On At Mumblesby?⋆
Plaster Sinners⋆
Blue Murder
One Man's Meat⋆
The Naked Nuns⋆
Broomsticks Over Flaxborough⋆
The Flaxborough Crab⋆
Charity Ends at Home
Lonelyheart 4122⋆
Hopjoy Was Here⋆
Bump in the Night⋆
Coffin Scarcely Used⋆

⋆ *also available in Methuen Paperback*

COLIN WATSON

Lonelyheart 4122

A Flaxborough Novel

A Methuen Paperback

A Methuen Paperback

LONELYHEART 4122
ISBN 0 413 55490 2

First published in Great Britain 1967
by Eyre & Spottiswoode Ltd
Copyright © 1967 by Colin Watson
This edition published 1984
and reprinted 1986
by Methuen London Ltd
11 New Fetter Lane, London EC4P 4EE

Printed and bound in Great Britain by
Richard Clay (The Chaucer Press) Ltd,
Bungay, Suffolk

Chapter One

ARTHUR HENRY SPAIN, BUTCHER, OF HARLOW PLACE, FLAX-borough, awoke one morning from a dream in which he had been asking all his customers how to spell 'phlegm' and thought – quite inconsequentially: I haven't seen anything of Lilian lately.

He nudged his wife.

'What do you reckon's up with Lil?'

'Up with her? What do you mean?'

'Well, she's not been round for ages.'

'She suits herself.'

'I've not seen her in the shop either.'

Mrs Spain pondered a moment. Then she shrugged away whatever thought had wriggled into her mind. 'Oh, you know what Lil is. Probably taken the huff about something.'

'I'll ask Mrs Maple.'

'Just as you like.'

Mr Spain did ask Mrs Maple. He had a word with Doris Bycroft, too. Then with the window cleaner from Cadwell Avenue. Quite casually, in the way of daily business. But none of them remembered having seen Mrs Lilian Bannister during the past two or even three weeks. Mr Spain resolved to call at her house on his very next early closing day.

He went there straight from the shop, thinking that lunch time would be the best occasion to find his sister-in-law at home; she was a stickler for her meals routine still, after nearly two years of widowhood.

He walked up the path of the small, semi-detached house in Cadwell Close and rang the bell. He waited and rang the bell again, this time without hope. Nothing happened. Mr Spain pushed back the flap of the letter box and peered in. A stair-

post, shiny brown lino, an oak hall stand – all neat, clean and
rather depressing.

Mr Spain unlatched the side gate and made his way to the
back of the house, glancing through the windows of the sitting
room, with its cold, bulgy leather suite; and of the kitchen, that
looked designed for the preparation of tinned salmon sand-
wiches and bedtime Horlicks and nothing else; until he arrived
at a door porched within a little glasshouse.

Here he experienced his first wave of real alarm. Ranged
tidily beneath a slatted wooden bench were more than a dozen
bottles of milk. The contents of those at the back were floc-
culent and tinged with a watery green.

He tried the door, found it locked as he had expected and
went back to the front.

A woman stood on the path, gazing up dubiously at the bedroom windows. She was a very ordinary looking woman,
middle-aged, dumpily dressed, bespectacled and hatted.

'Yes?' Mr Spain growled at her. He hadn't meant to sound
hostile, but the sight of the milk bottles had upset him.

The woman smiled nervously, then looked back at the house.
'There doesn't seem to be anyone in.'

'No, there isn't.'

'I've called several times.' A touch of complaint was in her
voice; it annoyed him.

'What for?'

'Well, to get in. It's mine – or it will be on the 25th. That's
what I. . . .'

'Yours?' Mr Spain's small eyes were nearly swallowed in a
scowl of incredulity.

'Yes, we've bought it. Me and my husband.'

It was true. Mr Spain went round to the estate agent whose
name, like scriptural authority, the woman had quoted in final
answer to his questioning. The agent confirmed that Mrs Bannister had asked him a couple of months ago to sell the house;
he understood that a contract had been signed and that posses-
sion was to be given within the next few days.

'What on earth is the woman up to?' Mr Spain asked his

wife over a delayed and somewhat acrimonious lunch. 'She never said anything to us.'

Mrs Spain cut savagely into a suet pudding.

'What did that agent have to tell you about it?'

'Nothing, really. They don't care, once the thing's off their books.'

'No, and I don't suppose he cares that there's nearly a hundred pounds of ours in that house.'

'Well, *he*'d not know about that, would he?'

'Who's the solicitor? She'd have to do it through a solicitor?'

'Scorpe, probably.'

She nodded imperatively. 'You can go and see him this afternoon.'

'Yes, but. . . .'

'Go and see him.'

Somewhat to Mr Spain's surprise, Mr Justin Scorpe obviously found his visit welcome. He was, he admitted, a trifle anxious about Mrs Bannister. One or two minor matters in connection with the sale remained to be cleared up, but his client did not seem to be available. No doubt Mr – ah – Spain was calling on his sister-in-law's behalf.

No, said Mr Spain, he wasn't. He just wanted to know where Lilian was hiding herself.

Mr Scorpe frowned. Hiding is not the word for which solicitors much care.

'But I know of no reason,' said Mr Scorpe, 'why Mrs Bannister should not be continuing to live at home until the date of completion. That is still a fortnight distant.'

'I don't even know why she's sold her house. No one does.'

Mr Scorpe examined him carefully for a moment over the top of heavy, blackframed spectacles.

'As a matter of fact,' said Mr Spain, 'I was rather hoping that you might have some idea.'

'Of her whereabouts?'

'Not only that. We'd like to know what she had in mind – what put her up to this business.'

'I cannot recollect her saying anything about reasons or intentions.'

'The fact is, my wife's a bit worried. I am, too. I mean, there's that milk. A whole lot of it. She's not taken it in.'

Mr Scorpe's bushy brows registered recognition of a classic forensic symptom. After a thoughtful silence he leaned a little closer to Mr Spain.

'Tell me,' he said, 'would you say that Mrs Bannister had been faced recently with some kind of – ah – financial obligation?'

Mr Spain shook his head.

'There is one point about this sale,' said the solicitor, 'which I think in the circumstances I ought to mention. It is this – though of course you must regard it as strictly confidential. When the contract was signed, I made an advance to your sister-in-law – at her request – of four hundred pounds against the purchase price. It is sometimes done, you know, provided we have confidence in the parties concerned. And in this case everything was straightforward – no outstanding mortgage or anything.'

Mr Spain swallowed. 'Actually, that's not quite true.' He saw the solicitor stiffen with alarm and raised a reassuring hand. 'No, what I mean is that when Jack died I lent Lilian enough to clear what she still owed the building society. About a hundred. We've not asked for it back.'

'I see.'

'But it makes things even more queer. I'm absolutely certain that Lilian wouldn't try to dodge. She's the kind who'd be round to pay a debt the same day as she got the money.'

Neither spoke for several seconds. Then Mr Scorpe cleared his throat portentously.

'I don't much care for the sound of those milk bottles,' he said.

Mr Spain listened obediently, then realized what had been meant.

'No.' He got up. 'I think I'd better. . . .'

Mr Scorpe nodded, his lips pursed most judiciously.

If Detective Inspector Purbright found Mr Spain's tale a little lacking in circumstantial drama, he gave no sign of impatience. Relatives, he knew, were never inclined to credit odd propensities in those who had become as unexcitingly familiar as hatstands. Family loyalty seemed to anaesthetize imaginations that would transform the homes of neighbours into bordellos and put a Crippen behind every other shop counter.

He just soldiered on, courteous and tactful.

'Now, what sort of friends had your sister-in-law, Mr Spain? Would you know anything about that?'

'Friends? Well, no one special, really. One or two of the women round about, I suppose.'

'You can't think of anyone with whom she might have gone to stay for a few days.'

'I can't. Nor can the wife. She's no relations that I know of except for us and some people in Kirby Street and I happen to know she's not been there.'

'How old is she? No, of course, you told me.' Purbright glanced at the notes on his knee. 'Forty-three. What's she like? You know – good-looking? Active?'

Mr Spain shrugged. Combining chivalry with accuracy was not going to be easy.

'I'd not call her a beauty, exactly. Quite nice, though. Quiet, but quite nice.'

That, reflected Purbright, was how Landru had liked them. And Mr Smith, with that bath of his. Aloud he said: 'You don't think Mrs Bannister had any intention of marrying again?'

'Oh, no.' The butcher seemed to find the possibility faintly indecent.

'She hasn't a friend who might have been expected to....' The inspector spread one hand in elegant inquiry, looked at Mr Spain's face and promptly changed tack.

'This money, now, Mr Spain. Do you suppose Mrs Bannister might simply have taken it into her head to go off on

holiday, something a bit extravagant, perhaps? That is sometimes a sudden temptation to people who haven't had much
excitement and feel maybe they should take the chance and
say nothing. After all, she had no ties.'

Mr Spain looked dubious. 'I had wondered, actually. But
Lilian's always been so methodical. It's that business of the
milk I can't get over. And I'm sure she would have let next
door know.'

'You asked them?'

'Sort of. Just casually. I didn't want to set anything off. You
know.'

Purbright rose. He was very tall, but a slow amiability of
manner prevented his height from being intimidating. Rather
did he have the endearing ungainliness of some outsize domestic animal.

He clipped together the notes he had made and smiled down
at Mr Spain.

'Perhaps we should let it ride for a few days longer. She
must know that she will have to be back in time to prepare for
the other people moving into the house. Of course, if she still
hasn't turned up by then we shall have to see what can be done
to trace her.'

'You don't think I'm making too much of all this? Mr
Scorpe said. . . .'

'No, you've been very sensible, Mr Spain. If you do think
of anything else I'd be glad to hear from you straight away.
Oh, and a photograph – that would be particularly helpful.'

As soon as his visitor had gone, the inspector opened a
drawer of the desk and took out a folder. Inside the folder were
two sheets of typescript and, attached to them, a photograph
of a woman of between thirty-five and forty. He reached for a
cup of half-cold tea and sipped it thoughtfully while he read
first the typewritten pages and then the notes of what he had
been told by the anxious butcher of Harlow Place.

Chapter Two

WHENEVER INSPECTOR PURBRIGHT WAS FACED WITH A SEEM-
ingly intractable problem, he took it to the chief constable,
Mr Harcourt Chubb. For one thing, it was only proper, pro-
fessionally, that he should. 'The correct channels' were much
revered by Mr Chubb and as long as he believed his sub-
ordinates were sailing them he could be relied upon to keep
safely on shore.

The other reason for consultation – and again aquatic simile
is useful – was that the chief constable had the sort of mind
which, because it was so static, aided reflection. By dropping
facts, like pebbles, into it and watching the ripples of pretended sapience spread over its calm surface, Purbright was
enabled somehow to form ideas that might not otherwise have
occurred to him.

So, when the final day of Mrs Bannister's legal occupancy of
her house had brought no sign of the missing vendor, Purbright took himself to the chief constable's office.

This was a large, cool room, the rather grand fireplace of
which had been preserved as a suitable leaning place for Mr
Chubb. The chief constable had never been known, save in
the most intimate domestic circumstances, to sit down.

'I'm afraid, sir,' Purbright began, 'that another lady has disappeared.'

Mr Chubb frowned. The connotation of 'another' eluded
him and he felt rather guilty about it.

'You'd better have a chair, Mr Purbright. That's right. Now
what have you come to tell me?'

Purbright recounted Mr Spain's story, together with what
he had been able to learn himself during the past few days of
Mrs Bannister's history and associations. This amounted to
very little.

'The last that anything was seen of the woman seems to have been around the end of last month. A window cleaner remembers calling and getting paid. He's been twice since then and he has the impression that everything in the rooms has stayed exactly as it was.'

'You mean he looks in?' Mr Chubb made it sound like an aberration.

'He's a very perceptive window cleaner, sir.' Purbright did not think it necessary to add that the man was a notable opportunist, too, being reputed to carry a mattress in his van for the accommodation of conquests.

'You've checked the hospitals, I suppose?'

'We did that last week. And Sergeant Love has covered the travel agencies. I'm having the woman's picture circulated and we're making inquiries at the railway and bus stations. Just as we did for Martha Reckitt.'

'Ah, yes,' said Mr Chubb. He was relieved of his fear that Purbright was going to leave him cluelessly clutching for the implications of that 'another'.

'We didn't get very far with that, Mr Purbright, did we?'

'We didn't get anywhere.'

'No.' Mr Chubb stroked his cheek and directed his sad, elder statesman gaze out of the window.

Purbright waited a moment and said : 'You'll have spotted the rather interesting parallels between the two cases.'

'Parallels. Yes. . . .'

'Both about the same age. Both rather retiring, without close friends, lonely perhaps. One a spinster – I use the word technically, sir; it's not one I like – and the other a widow. . . .'

'I don't like that one either,' broke in Mr Chubb gamely. 'Weeds.' He wrinkled his nose.

'Quite. What I'm getting at, though, is that perhaps the most significant thing they had in common – apart from some ready money – was availability.'

'Oh, I don't know about that, Mr Purbright. I would have thought them both pretty moral, from what you say. Martha especially; her mother was a very decent soul.'

'I mean matrimonially available.'

Mr Chubb nodded. 'I'm with you. Go on.'

'A woman who keeps a reputation for respectability in Flaxborough for forty years is not easily lured. I mean, she isn't
going to run off with the first man who knocks on the door and
tells her he wants her to do some modelling. She would need
to be offered a solid proposition, however romantic the trim-
mings. You will say that lust seethes within the most maidenly
bosom' – none knew better than Purbright that Mr Chubb
would say nothing of the sort – 'and you will be right. But
always there is this prime regard to security.'

'You talk of luring. We don't really know about that, though,
do we?'

'The only alternative is that Miss Reckitt and Mrs Bannister
went off on their own initiative, without a word to anybody,
leaving their belongings and obligations.'

'Such things do happen.' Mr Chubb pouted, wondering how
to redeem what he realized was a somewhat shallow observation. 'Change of life, you know,' he added mysteriously.

'Both a little young for the menopause, surely, sir?'

The chief constable let the point go.

'No, I agree with you that luring is the aspect that we must
concentrate on,' said Purbright shamelessly. 'The spontaneous
departure theory will hardly work for two cases in the same
town within so short a time. Can we have another look at your
point of view about both ladies having been matrimonially
available?'

'Your point, Mr Purbright.'

'I think we shall find that an offer of marriage has figured
at some stage in each case. It's the only bait I can think of that
would have worked in the circumstances.'

'So they might now be married?'

'Not unless they used false names. We did make the appropriate inquiries, you know.'

'In that case, I don't see that these hypothetical proposals
of marriage can be of much help to us, Mr Purbright. They are
scarcely likely to have been made before witnesses.'

'There could be written references to them. We know that neither of these women went out very much. Miss Reckitt's landlady said Martha was almost a recluse and Mrs Bannister certainly didn't share in any social whirls. It would be quite in character for a latter-day courtship to be conducted by correspondence. They'd both tend to be secretive, and a middle aged woman will often derive quite a lot of excitement from letter writing. Look at some of our poison pen customers.'

The chief constable stared gloomily at the middle of the floor as if he found in the carpet pattern a representation of human perversity. Yorkshire terriers – of which, to Purbright's abiding horror, Mr Chubb had nine – might have a wayward attitude to carpets but they did not post anonymous letters.

'You'll remember, sir,' Purbright was saying, 'that we found nothing in the way of a lead among Miss Reckitt's things, but we weren't likely to, anyway. The landlady had the impression that she kept all her letters in her handbag. I've more hopes of Mrs Bannister's place. She had the house to herself, so there was no need for her to worry about prying.'

'You know, Mr Purbright, you're quite an expert on female psychology. I trust you will never be tempted to turn it to nefarious account.'

The inspector accepted the pleasantry graciously and with some thankfulness. It meant that Mr Chubb had had his fill of information and theorizing for one day – perhaps for the week – and would be content to leave Purbright to get on with things in his own way.

He took his leave, collected Sergeant Love from the small, boot-loud canteen, and picked up from his desk the key, labelled by the scrupulous Mr Scorpe, to 4 Cadwell Close.

'It isn't one of those human remains things, is it?' the sergeant asked as they were driving along St Ann's Place.

'I sincerely hope not, Sid.'

Purbright was never quite sure whether Love's questions were prompted by timidity or morbid zest. The sergeant was by no means as young as he looked – if he were, he would be wearing a school cap. And he had that cherubic innocence of expression that usually betokens highly developed licentious-ness. But not, Purbright knew, in his case – his face was just his misfortune; he really was without vice. On the other hand, the innocent had the most extraordinary capacity for probing horrors. They could make pets of maggots and alleys of eye-balls.

The search of the house did not take very long. Reports of Mrs Bannister's neatness had not been exaggerated. Purbright and the sergeant first toured the rooms in turn. The bay windowed front room contained only a three-piece suite in brown leather cloth; a piano with very white keys and three framed photographs on its top; a highly polished but elderly wireless set; and a china cabinet occupied by a thick, gold-lustre coffee service, half a dozen sherry glasses and a pair of pink urns bearing arcadian views. In the living room were dining table and chairs, a fireside chair and a sideboard, older and heavier than the rest of the furniture. Purbright glanced briefly into its cupboards and three drawers. In the bottom drawer he glimpsed papers, books, envelopes.

'We'll come back to that in a minute, Sid.'

Two of the bedrooms were unfurnished, except for a bare bedstead and a marble washstand in the larger one. The third bedroom was obviously Mrs Bannister's. The pink satin counterpane over the made bed was uncreased but it bulged slightly near the top at one side. Purbright pulled back the covers. A folded nightdress lay beneath them.

Love opened the door of the mahogany wardrobe. Five dresses hung there, a black coat, two woollen skirts and a tweed costume. On the floor were four pairs of shoes. Pur-bright pushed back the door by which they had entered the room. He saw the blue dressing gown hanging from it. A moment later Love heard him moving in the bathroom across the landing, then he was back again.

'Toothbrush and toothpaste are still there,' Purbright said. He began looking through the chest of drawers.

'She can't have taken many of these, either. If any.'

Love felt faintly guilty as he watched the turning over of

stockings and blouses and underwear. The things were surprisingly brief and frilly. He somehow had expected long sleeved vests and bloomers in tans and butcher blue.

Then he saw the inspector pause in his search.

Purbright straightened up. He was holding three sheets of note-paper that he had found tucked beneath handkerchiefs. Each was a brief letter beginning: 'Lilian, My Dear....' None bore an address. Each was subscribed: 'Your Impatient Rex.'

Love looked admiringly at the way in which Purbright handled the letters; he had slipped on a pair of white cotton gloves.

'Thinking of prints, eh?' said Love.

'Dabs, Sid, surely. Do let's be professional.' He finished reading the first letter and put it gently on the counterpane. The sergeant looked down at the round, clear writing.

> Lilian, My Dear – I wonder if you can imagine how much our little stroll together meant to me. It is so true all that about 'sermons in streams and books in trees and good in everything'. At least, I see it is true when you are with me. Isn't the country marvellous? What a lot I was missing up there in my big Mayfair flat. Now I do nothing but dream of our little cottage. I am seeing the agent again tomorrow and I hope to have good news from my publisher before the end of the week. It is just this matter of the deposit that is a teeny bit awkward. But do not worry, my true one. We cannot have a Cloud in those clear eyes, can we?! Until Tuesday.
>
> Your Impatient Rex.

'Bloody hell,' muttered Sergeant Love.

Purbright raised his eyes. 'Ah, you've spotted the misquotation. If Rex is an author he'll have to do better than that.'

He placed the second letter on the bed.

> Lilian, My Dear – I took a trip, or pilgrimage should I say? to the church this morning. How right you are, what a noble edifice and how fitting for vows unto death. I think I

must use the scene for my next novel. Thank you for lending me back those earlier letters. I was right, I think, they do contain some phrases that ought to be worked into the book. You see what inspiration you give me!! And here is some good news. My publisher sent me a long telegram this morning begging me not to consider the offer from that big rival I told you about. He says he will personally send me two thousand pounds (think of that, Lilian!) out of his own private fortune if his other directors do not manage to raise the money before Settling Day, as they call it 'on Change' (you remember I told you about that). What a pity publishers are the slaves of the City these days. Art should be far above that sort of thing. Anyway, I tell you all this so you can feel easy about the little 'investment in our happiness' that you want to make. You will see that I am right when I say you have a 'business head' on those graceful shoulders!! By the way, the agent say that cash *will* be best – these 'country swains' are suspicious of cheques! Goodnight, a sweet goodnight, my dear. I will be waiting tomorrow at Our Tree. Your Impatient Rex. P.S. The agent also tells me that he thinks our 'enemy' will withdraw his bid for the cottage once our deposit is paid. Good-O!

The third letter was more brief.

Lilian, My Dear – Something has 'cropped up', as they say. That literary luncheon in Town has been brought forward to Wednesday. What a nuisance! but my publisher says it cannot be helped because J. B. Priestley couldn't manage Friday so you will understand I am sure. Come to Our Tree on Friday at seven and I shouldn't be surprised if I bring 'something special' from a certain merry goldsmith in Old London Town!!

Your Impatient Rex.

'Exit Mrs Bannister,' said Purbright. 'Via Our Tree.' He folded the letters and slipped them into an envelope before peeling off the white cotton gloves.

'He certainly writes like an author,' Love said. The inspector
gave him a shocked stare.

Downstairs, Purbright emptied the contents of the sideboard drawer upon the dining table. They consisted mainly of
household bills and receipts for small amounts, insurance
documents, old building society records, recipes snipped from
magazines, ageing snapshots and detergent circulars. In a
separate envelope was correspondence relating to the sale of
the house. There were also two bank statements covering a
fairly lengthy time and a cheque book with seven cheques remaining. Mrs Bannister clearly had not made frequent use of
her bank's services. All the better, thought Purbright.

He turned back the counterfoils, one by one. The upper-
most, dated a month previously, was marked 'Self', a withdrawal of four hundred pounds.

The 'investment in happiness', obviously.

There followed stubs recording payments to the borough
council – rates, presumably – and to such other unexciting
bodies as water and electricity boards, an insurance company
and a mail order house.

Only one counterfoil related to a transaction that could not
be immediately dismissed as orthodox.

Its date was four months old; the amount, twenty guineas;
the payee, Sylvia Staunch.

Purbright looked at it for several seconds. He turned to
Sergeant Love.

'Have *you* any notion, Sid, of who Miss or Mrs Sylvia
Staunch happens to be?'

Love pondered. He pulled at his smooth, pink, cherubic
cheek.

'It rings a bloody bell,' he said at last.

Chapter Three

FLAXBOROUGH. WHAT A NICE NAME. LONG BEFORE THE LONDON train pulled in behind the Gothic extravagance of Flaxborough station's façade – before even it had rumbled across points somewhere north of Derby and settled to a smooth pace on a lonely line towards the ever enlarging, ever brightening skies of eastern England – Miss Lucilla Teatime had decided that Flaxborough was going to be very much to her taste.

She was ready for a change, for a withdrawal from familiar places and the familiar round. That round, she warned herself, had been on the point of catching up with her lately. And if one wanted to preserve one's independence and interest in life, it didn't do to be caught up with.

A slight sense of disloyalty – a twinge, merely – had visited her with the decision to leave London for a while. She had spent nearly all her life there and with keen enjoyment. Her physical health remained excellent and she was fairly sure that she was as alert as ever. But she realized that she was not necessarily the best judge of that. There had been one or two occasions in the past year when a lapse of memory or of shrewdness had put her at a temporary disadvantage. In a way, she was thankful for them; they were timely signals of the danger of complacency.

Londoners, Miss Teatime reflected now in the cosy solitude of her first-class compartment, did tend to be complacent. It explained their gullibility. The cleverness one needed to be an active component of that vast turbulent city was so obvious that the possibility of being outsmarted was unthinkable. Hence the success of so many hard headed provincials in creaming off their fortunes in London before the natives realized that they hadn't come just for a football match and a look at the pigeons.

No, it would do her no harm to spend a spell away from dear, parochial old London. Her faculties needed a stretch. Something fresh, something challenging was indicated.

She looked out of the window. Huge rectangles of culti-vated land, bordered by long, cleft-like drains and low hedges, succeeded one another as far as the misty, blue-grey horizon. The clusters of farm buildings, lying at what seemed miles apart, looked clean and symmetrical and efficient. Not in the least picturesque. Miss Teatime thought of the farms pictured in television commercials for processed foods a⸍d smiled at the simple faith of the city dweller.

Not a smock in sight. The place seemed depopulated. Only the occasional scarlet flash of a tractor crawling over the black acres testified to human activity. She gazed to the landscape's indistinct, lavender-coloured rim. It was smudged with clumps of trees and spiked, here and there, with steeples – mere thorns they seemed against the vastness of the sky.

Miss Teatime picked up the book on the seat beside her. Barrington-Hoole's _Guide to Eastern England_. She began to glance through its illustrations and soon came to a scene that corresponded almost exactly with the view through the car-riage window. She felt pleased with herself and with the book too, and turned to the chapter on Flaxborough.

It confirmed what she had been told already: that Flax-borough was a market town of some antiquity with a remark-able record of social and political intransigence. The Romans had lost a legion there; the Normans had written it off as an incorrigible and quite undesirable bandit stronghold; while the Vikings – welcomed as kindred spirits and encouraged to settle – had fathered a population whose sturdy bloodyminded-ness had survived every attempt for eight centuries to sub-ordinate and absorb it.

Flaxborough was blessed, she read, with steady and well-founded prosperity. There was no reason to suppose that this would diminish while the town was surrounded by a thousand square miles of rich farming land. It had docks (its river, as the Vikings had been delighted to discover, was navigable) and food factories and a plastics industry.

Municipal tradition was colourful. Of the two hundred and five mayors who had held office since the extortion of a charter of incorporation from a hard-up sixteenth-century king, twenty-three had been knighted, one canonized (in genuine error, some historians claimed), six had risen to eminence in the New World and four had been hanged in the Old. To the borough's freemen still nominally belonged the privilege of emptying a chamber pot from the balcony of the Assembly Rooms once a year on the mayor's birthday, but the requirement of there being marshalled beneath 'twelve able-bodied paupers of the parish' had fallen into desuetude. Not so the observance of the ceremony of 'pudding tussle'. There were still, apparently, plenty of willing contestants in this curious All Souls' Day version of a football match, in which a ring of black pudding was booted to disintegration in the Market Place – symbolic, said wishfully thinking antiquarians, of a communal intolerance of maidenheads.

By the time she had absorbed all this and more, equally stimulating information, about the town she had elected to visit, Miss Teatime became aware of a change in the rhythm of the train's wheels. It had slowed and become disjointed. She looked up. A water tower and a warehouse glided by, followed by a dilapidated engine shed. Trucks crowded up to the window and fell away again with a noise like the clucking of iron poultry. Across the emptiness of a goods yard she glimpsed pantiled roofs, red in the sun as country apples, and beyond them a church tower, honey-sunned and sharply tangible in clear air.

'Saint Laurence's,' murmured Miss Teatime, happily confident.

She carried her two cases, which were not heavy enough to be troublesome, across the high, arched foot bridge and past the ticket office. She gave her ticket and a warm smile to the man leaning casually by the window. He looked more like a sailor than a railwayman. His calm, appraising stare followed her out of the booking hall. For her age, Lucy Teatime was remarkably trim and handsome. People instinctively approved of her, for there was in her appearance the flattering suggestion that she had taken pains to spare one personally the spectacle of yet another dumpy, disgruntled, defeated old woman.

For her part, she regarded self preservation (short of courting grotesqueness) to be as much a public duty as a private pleasure. Decrepit bodies were no less offensive than decrepit buildings; tasteless clothes as inexcusable as ugly shop fronts. There ought to be inspectors, she told herself sometimes, with power to demand the production of a lipstick or to serve a bosom restitution order.

Outside the station she looked round for a taxi, then changed her mind. London habit was here an extravagance, almost an eccentricity. One could walk without being mown down, so why not? Anyway, there wasn't a taxi in sight.

She crossed the station square and began walking up the narrow lane that opened from it and led to where she could see an intersecting stream of cars and buses. This, she remembered from the guide map, would be East Street, at the other end of which was the Roebuck, the hotel she had selected for no better reason than that of liking its name.

East Street was a much busier thoroughfare than she had anticipated. It did not justify her optimism in regard to pedestrian safety. The footpath was about three feet wide, a mere ledge from which one was in constant danger of being extruded into the wheeled torrent. It was only when Miss Teatime found opportunity to look into the faces of her fellow walkers and see there either bland indifference or, just as often, a lively amusement at the expressions of desperately braking drivers, that she took courage from the discovery that the whole thing was really a game – a contemporary version of bear-baiting. She relaxed a little and turned part of her attention to the shops.

After a while, the street and the pavement widened and the congestion eased. There were space and time to stare around. Miss Teatime noticed a cinema and a Woolworth's and a self service store plastered with the slogans of twopence-off evangelism. Not so different from Twickenham after all, she reflected. Then she looked up to the surmounting buildings and saw the dignified, gracious face of the eighteenth century. For the whole length of the street, these Georgian façades had survived and there was now an air of almost jaunty self-congratulation about their new coats and bright pastel colour-wash.

For some reason, the road was empty of traffic – it had probably coagulated at the scene of some particularly rash act of pedestrian provocation farther back. Miss Teatime crossed over. She had spotted a short row of market stalls. They proved disappointing. No piles of miraculously undervalued coach lamps, paper weights and copper kettles. Just garden plants, dress materials, cut-price sweets. Again her optimism sagged. But she was learning, she told herself; she'd soon have the measure of the place.

While standing still by the plant stall, she noticed a man cleaning a first floor window a few yards farther along. A bucket stood near the foot of the ladder. His barrow, on which rested another ladder, was in the gutter. She glanced at the barrow idly and again at the window cleaner. Then, incredulous, she stared at the barrow once more. In bold white letters along the side was proclaimed: THE QUEEN MUST MAKE WATER.

Miss Teatime looked covertly at passers-by to see if they, too, had seen the astounding message. None gave any sign of finding it unusual. Only one, a boy who had slipped from a group of companions, seemed at all concerned. Keeping one eye on the window cleaner, he walked warily past the ladder and let something fall from his hand into the bucket. Then he doubled back to his friends and stood with them, watching.

Soon afterwards, the man came down from the window. He had a pale, bird-like face and quick, worried eyes. He knelt by the bucket and plunged his leather into the water, swirling it about while he looked up and down the street like a nervous sentry. He withdrew the leather and with a single ferocious twist wrung it out.

The effect was horrible. From between his fingers there

gushed and squirted blood.

Miss Teatime gave a little squeal. The man glared at her, then looked down. With a bellow of dread he sprang to his feet, dropped the encarmadined leather and staggered across the pavement.

'The grape!' he howled. 'The accursed grape!'

Miss Teatime heard a tut of disapproval from the woman behind the stall. 'It's too bad of those boys. They'll have him off his ladder one of these days.'

A packet of dye. Of course. She felt a bit cross at having squealed.

'They tease him, do they?' she said to the stallholder.

'Well, he's got a thing about drink, you know,' the woman explained. 'Religious.'

'Ah,' said Miss Teatime.

The man had recovered himself sufficiently to kick the bucket into the roadway. Muttering, he watched its contents drain away. Then he packed ladders and bucket on the barrow and swung it round in order to depart. Miss Teatime saw revealed on its other side the second half of his proclamation:
... OUR ONLY DRINK BY LAW.

'I hope,' she said five minutes later to the girl in the reception office of the Roebuck, 'that this is not a temperance hotel. The point hadn't occurred to me when I booked.'

'Oh, no, madam. We're fully licensed.'

'Excellent. In that case perhaps you would be good enough to have a little whisky sent to my room. Also a copy of the local paper, if you don't mind.'

She went upstairs, accompanied by a chambermaid carrying her cases. The room, she saw with instant pleasure, overlooked the river. Through the net-curtained casement she glimpsed the tops of masts and the jib of a dock crane; it looked like the neck of an inquisitive dinosaur. The small bed had a frilled cover, white, with a wealth of fat pink roses. There was a matching armchair beside the gas fire. A pot of white cyclamen stood on a little table in the centre of the room. At the foot of the bed was one of those curious slatted stools, of uncertain purpose, that are found only in English hotel rooms, and in a corner was the inevitable plywood wardrobe that sways and emits the hollow rattle of hangers when one first tries to open the door but which, once broached, can never again be closed.

Miss Teatime had a brief, maidenly wash, changed her dress and shoes, and pulled the chair nearer the window. She had just sat down after looping back the curtain when the girl from the reception office arrived with a glass of whisky and a newspaper. Miss Teatime noted approvingly that the whisky was a double.

'Did you feel faint after the journey, madam?' The girl held the glass like a medicine measure.

'Not a bit of it. Cheers!'

The girl withdrew, looking slightly bewildered.

For a while, Miss Teatime watched the dark water of the river slipping by below. It flowed through a canyon of warehouse walls. They were of some kind of stone, pale cinnamon streaked with sage, and pierced high above the water line by dark apertures with gently rounded tops. From some of these jutted timber gallows. The ceaseless wheeling of gulls superimposed on the scene a fluid pattern of flashing white.

She turned at last from the window, finished her drink, and unfolded the *Flaxborough Citizen*.

It was a voluminous paper that tented the small woman in the armchair. She made a quick survey of its general contents, then folded it back at the second page of classified advertisements. This contained a Situations Vacant section and a Personal column.

With a pencil Miss Teatime ringed three advertisements under Situations. All were for companions.

Next she took from one of her cases the *Flaxborough Street Directory and Gazetteer* which she had received by post a fortnight before. She looked up three names and addresses and turned three times to the town map. What she inferred from these references did not, apparently, impress her. She scribbled through the pencilled rings and began to explore the Personal column.

It was not promising.

Most of the entries were purely commercial advertisements, couched in pert or whimsical terms. Thus: 'A.D. – Meet me at the Flaxborough Pram Mart, Tuesday, and we'll choose our Bargain together. They have fabulous easy terms. – Daisy.'

Or: 'Don't beef, come to Hambles, West Row, where they have the finest meat in town.'

The blandishments of money lenders were much in evidence. 'From ten to ten thousand pounds' was to be had at the drop of a postcard, and with no security. Miss Teatime smiled to herself. She knew that the 'no security' was intended to qualify the borrower's legal position, not the loan.

Here, too, was the hunting ground of the hawkers of such curious boons as foolproof chimney cowls, denture fixatives ('spare yourself shame'), cures for stuttering and means to learn the mandolin in a week.

She was admonished in turn to learn the secrets of the Rosicrucians, provide herself with the powers of Joan the Wad and avoid furs got by torture.

Then came a wide selection of addresses from which, under plain cover, unspecified artifacts in rubber would be promptly dispatched. 'Good old thousand per cent and no overheads,' murmured Miss Teatime to herself.

Her eye travelled down.

'Unparalleled opportunity for lovers of unusual art. . . .'

Good God! Maisie and Ted were still at it. The same, exactly. Real old troupers.

'A business opening exists. . . .' Oh, no. Not that one.

'Gentleman who has written novel about exciting war experiences would appreciate advice as to having same published.' Better. But still only as a last resort. Alas, those gentlemen from the war. . . .

Ah!

Right at the bottom of the column, it was. Something for which she had not dared to hope. Not in remote, prosperous, hard headed Flaxborough.

A matrimonial bureau.

Well, what else could be meant by 'Handclasp House: Are you weary of the solitary path?'

Miss Teatime read the whole advertisement through carefully. Clients from all walks of life ... introductions arranged ... view to permanent association ... countless instances of happiness ... small initial fee.... There was no doubt about it.

She took from her handbag a little lavender-coloured memorandum book. As she jotted down the address of Handclasp House, a smile spread over her face, illuminating charmingly its lineaments of good breeding.

Then she put the book away, folded the *Flaxborough Citizen* and resumed her contemplation of the waterside and the circling gulls.

Chapter Four

'TEASHOPS, SID,' INSPECTOR PURBRIGHT HAD SAID. 'I'VE A feeling that Miss Reckitt and Mrs Bannister would have chosen to be courted in teashops. Try taking their pictures round.'

There were eight establishments in Flaxborough that the sergeant felt he could reasonably include in his list, although two were in fact self service cafeterias and a third brashly advertised itself as a 'Shake 'n' Donut Bar'. These three he was able to eliminate within half an hour, but as he began to slog round the others he saw that he was in for a long and daunting quest.

In 'Penny's Pantry', next to the Guildhall, he waited for what seemed hours, wedged amidst elbows and enormous shopping baskets, while the sole attendant – Penny herself, he presumed – served customers who constantly replaced themselves like Hydra's heads. Each of these women appeared to have been forewarned of a long siege: she indicated cake after cake, which Penny loaded with gloomy fastidiousness into cardboard boxes.

When at last Love found himself within gesturing distance of the woman behind the counter and had managed to catch her eye, he raised his brows invitingly and jabbed a finger in the direction of a doorway through which he had noticed a number of unoccupied tables.

Not open, the woman mimed. *Eleven*. She turned to fork-lift an Almond Dainty out of the window.

I want a word with you, Love silently but urgently mouthed as soon as she glanced again in his direction.

She frowned. *What about?* her mouth framed.

It was like a conversation between two acute laryngitis patients.

I'm a po-lice off-i-cer, went Love's lips.

He saw the woman consider, nod brusquely, then disappear. He pushed his way to the side of the shop and went through into the tearoom. The woman was already there. She looked offended.

'We're very busy, you know.'

'Yes, I'm sorry, but I'll not keep you.' He took out his two photographs.

'I just want to know if you've seen either of these ladies here in the café at any time. In the last two or three months, anyway.'

She took a long, grave look.

'What have they done?'

'Nothing,' said Love, blandly. His blue eyes met her glance of disbelief and remained steady.

She held Mrs Bannister's picture. 'It might have been this one who was in the other week. I'm not sure, mind.'

'How long ago?'

'A fairish while. Two or three weeks. If it was her.' She started. 'Look, I'll have to get back to the shop.'

'All right. But can you remember who she was with?'

'Oh, but really. . . .' She thrust the photograph back into his hand and turned.

'It's important. Honestly.'

Relenting, she paused and stared at a table in the far corner. She seemed to seek there some left-behind impression. Love watched her face cloud with the effort of recollection, then saw a small smile.

'Dicky bow,' she said suddenly.

'I beg your pardon?'

'He was wearing one of those dicky bow ties. You don't often see them nowadays. That's all I remember, though.'

'Nothing else?'

She shook her head, but her gaze did not leave the corner table.

'How old was he?' Love asked.

'So-so. Middle aged, I suppose. Like her.'

'Hair?'

She shrugged.

'Dark? Fair?'

'Fair. He was....'

'Yes?'

'Well, I'm not sure how to describe it. Rather gall*ant*.' She stressed the second syllable. Purbright would have diagnosed from this slight flippancy a desire to be thought more level-headed than she really was. Love suffered from no such devious process of thought.

'What, a bit of a fancy lad, you mean?'

'Sort of,' she said, and departed.

The sergeant drew no results at all from 'The Pewter Kettle', a fearsomely hag-ridden chintzery in St Ann's Place, or from the Church Tower Restaurant. At 'The Honey Pot', he had to contend with a good deal of indignation from a maiden proprietress who was unshakeably convinced that he had come to accuse her of peddling purple hearts. The Clock Tea Rooms, in Market Street, he found to be closed for re-decoration.

It was his last call, at an unnamed first-floor café near the bus station, that produced the only response to the photograph of Martha Reckitt. A plump Italian girl, whose pneumatic occupancy of her waitress's frock gave her the appearance of the maid in a stage farce, recognized the picture at once.

'She come the day I start. Maybe the first, second customer.'

'That's why you remember her?'

'Sure.'

'Was she with anyone?'

'Yes. A man. I think a priest.'

Love looked surprised. 'A priest?' In his limited religious experience the word had an exotic ring. He had a fleeting vision of a figure in voluminous robes pouring tea like sacrificial wine.

'I think so. Very dark clothes and hands like so.' She joined the tips of her fingers. 'And all the time he is looking very sad at my legs.'

'Oh, you mean a clergyman,' Love said.

'I think. Yes.'

'Can you describe him?'

The girl pouted doubtfully. Oo, you little smasher, said the sergeant to himself.

'A man,' she said. 'Not young. Not as young as you.' Love glowed. 'But with a ... a something – you know?' Had *he* a something, the sergeant wondered, hoping very much that he had.

'Is there anything else you can think of? Colour of eyes or hair?'

'Oh, yes. Not dark hair. Colour like. . . .' She rippled fingers in the air, seeking a comparison within what vocabulary she had acquired, then brightened. 'Like chips!'

Purbright seemed quite pleased with his sergeant's report.

'You've gathered more than I expected, Sid. I wish I had your way with women.'

'I wouldn't have thought the descriptions were much help.'

'They seldom are, unless they include six-inch scars or a club foot. The point is that we now have a much clearer idea of the *kind* of man we're looking for – his line of business.'

'A clergyman who writes books, you mean?'

'Not at all. What we have to find is a non-clergyman who doesn't write books.'

'That ought to be easy,' said Love, hoping he was keeping his end up in the matter of trading ironies.

'Not easy,' Purbright qualified, 'but less difficult in the context of Flaxborough society than looking for, say, an embezzler or a fornicator. A needle is much simpler to find in a haystack than in a bin of other needles.

'Now then, whoever won the affections of Miss Reckitt and Mrs Bannister is obviously a professional or semi-professional con man. Among these people there is quite narrow specialization. The bogus charity collector does not cross into the territory of the encyclopaedia salesman. Nor does the inventor in need of capital to market his everlasting petrol capsule work overtime as a spirit guide.'

'Remember that bloke,' Love interrupted, 'who was supposed to have put old Alderman Wherry in touch with Edward the Seventh?'

'Just so,' said the inspector. 'A full-timer. They hung eighty-three taken-into-considerations on him.

'But to get back to the business in hand. Here we have another kind of full-timer. The con man who's forever pointed towards an altar. He's probably the hardest worker of them all. Think of a life that is perpetual courtship of the last woman on earth you'd care to marry. That's real graft, Sid.'

Sergeant Love, who was finding even his own restricted and unambitious wooing a bit of a strain from time to time, looked suitably awed.

'So you see we are not looking for an ordinary criminal,' Purbright went on. 'We seek a man who can pose convincingly as an author, probably as a clergyman, and possibly as other romantic things. It would be interesting to know what he is at the moment.'

'A surgeon,' suggested Love, a quick learner.

'Aye, very likely. Plenty of tuck in his jacket sleeve to show off long, sensitive hands, and a sprinkle of Dettol behind the driving seat.'

'What about a secret agent?'

Purbright looked dubious. 'Strictly for mentally retarded shop girls, I would have thought. Our man's a cut above trading on the Bond syndrome.'

'Clever,' Love said, 'the way he covered his tracks by getting those letters back from Mrs Bannister.'

'Quite. And we've got precious little from the three he *didn't* recover. Not even a print, apparently. I wonder how they corresponded between meetings. Without his having to give his address away, I mean.'

'Through some sort of box number, maybe. Could have been the post office.'

'Box number....' Purbright murmured. For some reason, the thought of twenty-one pounds insinuated itself. Twenty guineas. The professional touch. Guineas. Fee. Client.

'Sid,' he said suddenly, 'isn't there one of those matrimonial agencies somewhere in town?'

The question seemed to take a second or two to register. Then Love straightened in his chair.

'That name....'

'What name?'

'On the cheque. Stench ... Staunch.' He snapped his fingers. 'That's it – she runs a marriage bureau thing somewhere in Northgate. Where the Liberal Club used to be.'

Purbright rewarded the sergeant with a beam of affability, then looked at his watch. 'I'll go over now. What do you think I ought to ask for, a catalogue?'

Northgate was one of Flaxborough's more run-down thoroughfares. Older people could remember when it had been 'select' – the preserve of the kind of shopkeepers who saw their customers to the door and sent accounts headed 'Bot. of....' At one time as many as four of its tall, double-fronted houses had been graced with the brass plates of doctors. No inn had ever been suffered there, and no chapel either, for Northgate's residents and men of business held in equal abhorrence the vulgarity of public victualling and Methodism's shrill abstinence. It was a street in which one could picture the aristocratic chemists having actually made up prescriptions from the great jars of gilded porcelain and the gigantic tincture bottles in their windows. There would have been a traffic in hat boxes and packets of gingerbread and Gentlemen's Relish on the way home to side doors lettered in enamel *No Hawkers: No Circulars*.

But all that was long ago. With the shift of the town's commercial axis to East Street on the other side of the river, first prosperity and then dignity had drained from Northgate like sap from a tree. The doctors had departed and their mansions had become tenements or the offices of car accessory firms. Behind the engrimed bow windows of chemists and saddlers and confectioners, there went on the dark labour of cycle repairers and the renovators of sofas. The premises of what once had been the town's most magnificent provisions store now housed on one floor a refrigeration plant and some tons of frozen fish fingers and on the others the biggest stockpile of bottled sauce east of Manchester. As for the ban, so long sustained, upon Nonconformists and their bleak, hideous architecture, revenge had been taken by the enlargement with corrugated iron and match-boarding of the former carriage house of old Doctor Sanderson into a mission hall, complete with neon cross and posters that repeated the more offensive remarks of Old Testament prophets.

It was the baleful keening of the mission's congregation (its apparently permanent session embraced the rarest intervals of silence) that droned through the thin walls to Purbright's ear as he entered Northgate from Farrier Street. Drawing nearer its source, he wondered why religion – the western kind, anyway – laid such stress upon giving God praise. Never sympathy.

He crossed the road. It was pleasant to be warmed by the late afternoon sunshine and the inspector did not hurry. He did not despise seedy streets. Each had points of interest peculiar to itself. In Northgate there was a herbalist's, for instance. He stopped at the narrow, dark window, and peered at the little piles of crumbled leaves and crushed root set out on kitchen saucers, each with a hand written reference to the organic effect promised. Especially intriguing was the card against slippery elm. 'Makes delicious blancmange and is invaluable to the Family Planner (instructions over the counter).'

Farther along was a tobacconist's. A row of tiny snuff bottles bore such names as Seven Dials, Senator, Barbara's Muff, Voltaire and Pillycock. There was a photograph of Edgar Wallace above six dusty, foot-long cigarette holders looped to a display card. 'The Latest Novelty,' proclaimed a ticket on a pipe fashioned in the likeness of a can-can dancer's leg.

He glanced into another window and wondered what possible trade could be represented by the display there of a

potted geranium, a hank of clothes line and a carton containing two dozen bottles of syrup of figs. Its air of surrealism
was not dispelled by the printed announcement, gummed to
the glass: Wardrobes Bought.

'Morning, brother.'

Purbright turned. A thin, black-clad figure perched on a
bicycle was wobbling over the road towards him.

'Good afternoon, Mr Leaper.'

The cyclist wore a clerical collar but he was obviously very
young. He alighted and acknowledged Purbright's correction
with a half smile and a quick, nervous nod. Although he gave
the impression of being eager about something, he ventured no
further remark, but stood holding his handlebars and staring
at the front tyre.

'Lovely in the sun,' Purbright said, and began to walk on.

'Yes,' said Leaper. 'I've still some calls to do.'

The inspector watched him bend to his peddling and rapidly
disappear up the street. He was sceptical about the calls. The
Reverend Leaper's charge was, in fact, the Eastgate mission,
and *its* communicants were never anywhere else to be called
on. 'Out for a breather, I suppose,' Purbright concluded.

After a few more minutes' walk, he reached a part of the
pavement that broadened back to where a four storeyed building stood on its own. Tall railings flanked the three steps that
led to double doors standing open in the shelter of a stone
portico.

This was, or rather once had been, the Flaxborough Radical
Club. It was said that Mr Gladstone had cut a rose from the
bush that still grew in the little earth enclosure beside the
steps.

Just inside the doors was a list of the offices above. Purbright looked vainly for the name Staunch or reference to a
matrimonial agency. Then he noticed at the far end of the
stone-flagged entrance hall an illuminated sign. It hung over a
doorway and bore two words in bright green Gothic lettering
on a pink ground.

'Handclasp House'.

Chapter Five

PURBRIGHT PUSHED OPEN THE DOOR. HE ENTERED A SMALL square room, carpeted from wall to wall in dark grey. A paler, pinkish grey was the colour of the hessian-like material that covered the walls. There hung from the ceiling a plain white globe. Three chairs in mushroom plastic were the only furniture. The place was like an optician's waiting room – neutral, reticent.

Set diagonally across the far corners of the square were two more doors. A little orange bulb glowed in the centre of each. Purbright approached the door on his right. Like the other, it bore a notice.

When this light is on, MR DONALD STAUNCH is at the service of any gentleman who wishes to know how we can work to help him. Come straight in and make yourself at home.

He crossed to the other door, and read:

When this light is on, the free and friendly advice of MRS SYLVIA STAUNCH is available to our lady callers. Don't knock: come in and have a chat with her.

Clever, thought Purbright. He could not have devised a better formula himself to avoid the unfortunate ambiguity of merely labelling the doors 'Ladies' and 'Gentlemen'.

Perhaps in the circumstances he ought to have a word with Donald first. He opened the right hand door and stepped through.

The contrast to the aseptic waiting room was almost startling.

In the light from a tall standard lamp behind a cushion-strewn oaken settle, the inspector saw what might have been a stage set for an English domestic comedy. Two armchairs separated by a coffee table faced a glazed hearth in which glowed the dummy embers of an electric fire. Upon a sideboard were glasses, decanter, biscuit barrel and miniature dinner gong. An open work-basket was beside one armchair, a rush stool by the other. He saw somewhere a pipe lying in an ashtray, a small scattering of hair curlers, a magazine open at the picture of a nude. The smell of the room seemed to be compounded of flowers and fresh laundry, with just a suggestion of . . . he sniffed – yes, newly baked bread.

Clever, he said again to himself. Very. Even the versatile 'Rex' must have been a little awed by the insight and ingenuity of the Staunches.

'Do sit down, Mr er. . . .'

He turned.

There had entered by a door on the farther side of the fireplace a woman with bluish grey hair, expertly waved and lustered, and the glint around neck and wrists of rather a lot of jewellery. Her eyes were strong and alert.

'Purbright,' he supplied. 'Detective Inspector.'

Her smile narrowed for an instant to a pout. It emphasized her precise but heavy application of lipstick. Then the expression of businesslike solicitude was back.

She sat and ventured the small joke that seemed a proper way of getting a measure of the policeman's attitude.

'I presume you are not here to offer yourself as a client, inspector.'

Purbright smiled back. 'Hardly.'

'I thought not. You don't look married, and that is the surest sign that you have a wife and are well content with her.'

'I shall tell Mrs Purbright that.'

He saw, now that she was seated, that the tailoring of her clothes was excellent. She had slim, rather hard-looking legs.

'You are Mrs Staunch, of course?'

She inclined her head.

'I'd rather expected' – Purbright indicated the door by which he had entered – 'that it would be Mr Staunch whom I would find.'

'A small deception of the trade, inspector. I have a husband, but so far as the agency is concerned Donald is a fiction. I interview all my clients myself. It's just that men seem to find the first step easier if they think they're going to deal with a man. Once the ice is broken, they're quite happy to pour out their troubles to me.'

'Your husband takes no part in the work then?'

'In *this* work? Heavens, no. He has far too much of his own. In any case, I'm afraid Donald doesn't approve. He has the traditional English middle-class attitude to matrimonial agencies. Terribly *infra dig*.'

'Yet in no other country are people so insistent on the importance of being introduced. Isn't that just your function? To effect introductions?'

Mrs Staunch spread her hands. 'Precisely!' Her smile implied that she found Purbright a very sensible fellow indeed. 'But you try telling that to an architect!' She deepened her voice on the last word in mock solemnity.

'Architect?'

'Donald. Well, an architectural consultant, actually. Next time you want your cells rebuilding, or whatever, send for Donald. He did a prison block once.'

'It is your help rather than your husband's for which I should be obliged at the moment, Mrs Staunch.'

She bent forward attentively. 'Of course.'

'There are two women – both of them live here in Flax-borough, or have done up to recently – whom we are rather anxious to trace. One is a widow. The other is an unmarried woman. We think that they may have approached your agency, probably within the last six months or so.'

'You mean these women have disappeared?'

'In effect, yes. Certainly some of the relatives are worried and no one has been able to suggest any likely reason why either should have left home.'

Mrs Staunch reached for a note pad that was lying on the coffee table. 'You'd better give me their names.'

'Mrs Lilian Bannister – she's the widow, of course – and the other one's called Martha Reckitt.' He leaned forward and put two photographs on the table. Mrs Staunch finished writing and picked them up.

She looked at Purbright. 'You think about six months ago?'

'In Mrs Bannister's case, four exactly.'

She frowned. 'Why "exactly"?'

'That was the date on a cheque for twenty guineas which she made out to you.'

'Is it because of that cheque that you came to see me?'

'Because of the counterfoil, actually. At the moment we don't know that the cheque reached you.'

'Oh, it did.' Some of Mrs Staunch's affability seemed to have evaporated. She spoke quietly and with care. 'Mrs Bannister paid her registration fee and used the services of my agency for several weeks. I'm fairly sure that the other lady was a client as well – I'll have a look in my records in a moment. The trouble is. . . .' She paused.

Purbright watched her stroke the edge of one of the pictures reflectively with a long, puce-varnished fingernail.

'Tell me if I'm jumping too far ahead, inspector, but I can see that you believe something has happened to these women. Which leads you – naturally – to suppose some kind of criminal is responsible. Which in turn gives you the idea that they might have met him, or them, through the agency. Am I right?'

'I wouldn't quite. . . .'

'You might as well be frank, inspector. I certainly intend to be.'

'All right. That's roughly the argument so far.'

She nodded. 'Now let me tell you something of how this sort of agency operates. I want you to see certain difficulties that probably haven't occurred to you.

'In the first place, it is terribly important for people who come here to feel that the whole thing is strictly confidential. It is this that forces us to adopt certain forms of procedure that you might think – well – childish, melodramatic. My husband thinks it's awful; he calls it M.I.5 for the lovelorn.

What he doesn't understand is that you have to sort of cage lonely people up before you can do anything for them – it's safety they really want. And that means secrecy.

'Right. Someone comes along. Mrs Bannister, say. I list as much as she'll tell me about herself – age, hobbies, tastes, what she admires in a man. . . .'

'Financial means?' Purbright put in.

Mrs Staunch shrugged. 'If it seems relevant, yes. Anyway, all these things go down on the office record and she's allocated a number. That number is her guarantee of remaining anonymous right up to the time when she herself decides to reveal her identity to the person she believes she can be happy with.

'The next step is for me to prepare a selection from the gentlemen's file of clients who seem likely – in temperament, background, and so on – to match up with Mrs Bannister. This is where you have to be a bit of a psychologist, of course. And one has to bear in mind that it's opposites that often prove to agree best.

'Once I have let her have this selection – with numbers, not names, remember – it is up to her to write to any of them and suggest correspondence. All letters come to my office for re-direction, or to be collected, just as the clients prefer. So even I don't know who writes to whom. Sometimes people actually marry without my being any the wiser, though most are only too anxious to share their good news with me. I've had some very touching letters.'

Mrs Staunch paused briefly for reflection. Then she accepted the cigarette Purbright offered her and went on.

'Of course, Mrs Bannister would have what you might call a double chance. In addition to being given that list of "Possibles", she would have her number and details circulated to those of my gentlemen clients I considered might be interested in *her*. And if any proved to be so, their letters would reach her through the office here without her being put under any obligation.'

Purbright considered a while. 'There seems to be quite a

lot of work entailed. For you, I mean.' He forebore from adding: And no small loot, at twenty guineas a shot.

Mrs Stauch lowered her eyes and examined the hem of her skirt. 'It's tremendously worth while. It really is.'

'I think I'm beginning to see the difficulties you mentioned,' Purbright said.

'In relation to this inquiry of yours?'

'Yes. The field's a good deal wider than I would like. In my uninstructed optimism, I'd thought in terms of single, specific introductions. I hoped for a name and address for my pains.'

'Life is not simple, Mr Purbright.'

'No, indeed, Mrs Staunch. It takes all sorts, doesn't it?'

She glanced at him sharply, but his face was quite expressionless.

'Perhaps,' she said, rising, 'you'd better come along to my office. I want to be as helpful as I can. And if those poor women really have come to some harm. . . .'

'I'm afraid everything points that way.'

'Then naturally we must see what can be done. Provided' – she paused on her way to the door – 'you understand that anything I can tell you must be in the strictest confidence.'

Unsure of what this was supposed to mean, Purbright nodded gravely and followed her.

The office was a very small room with walls colour washed in primrose. On a wooden table were a typewriter, a letter basket and a hand operated duplicator. A dozen or so unopened letters were tucked behind tapes pinned to a board on the wall.

Mrs Staunch opened a drawer in the metal filing cabinet that stood in one corner. She took out a folder, referred to the note she had made earlier, and found after some searching a second folder.

She withdrew from each a form which she laid on the table before Purbright.

'There you are. Miss Reckitt and Mrs Bannister. I thought they would both be still on file.' She indicated hand written entries. 'They fill these in themselves. Here, you see . . . age, address, what they like doing, various personal details. . . .' She looked up. 'Any use?'

The inspector read through the firm, well formed back-hand of Martha Reckitt and then the less certain writing of the widow, spidery and laboured and with an occasional spelling mistake.

Martha claimed to be of respectable, religious family, the deaths of whose other members had left her lonely but reason-ably well provided with means for setting up a home of her own if she could meet someone sincere and companionable. She was interested in welfare work and thought she would like to live in the country; parish affairs greatly appealed to her. She had a fondness for needlework and reading, liked animals (her present situation, unfortunately, did not permit her to keep pets), and sometimes took a Sunday school class. Although tolerant in most manners, she could have no admiration for a man who drank. She did not condemn smoking – not pipe smoking anyway – but cared nothing for it herself. She had been told that she cooked well and was reasonably good look-ing. She enjoyed good health, apart from a slight asthmatic tendency.

Mrs Bannister made no mention of family other than a loyal reference to having lately lost 'one of the best'. Her consolations were the television, plays especially, and keeping her home nice. Nice, too, was her figure and often she thought she would like to see it in a dance frock again if the chance offered, which she hoped it would even now. She did lots of reading, loving books as she did and being a bit on the quiet side. Her special ambition, though, was to keep chickens and she would not hesitate to sell up her nice home for the sake of moving to a cottage in the country. What she would like in a man was attentiveness and a free and easy way, also educa-tion – that she admired very much.

When he had finished reading, Purbright put the sheets down and regarded them silently. Nothing, he thought, was so saddening as the conflict between fear and loneliness. It could be terribly dangerous, too.

'Tell me, Mrs Staunch – isn't there a real possibility of

people exploiting an agency like yours? I mean, here are two women who are obviously just asking for trouble.'

'You're thinking of what they have put down here about their means?'

'Certainly.'

'Ah, but things like that are just for my guidance. They're absolutely confidential. I never pass them on with introductions.'

'But there is no guarantee that these women won't divulge details themselves once a correspondence gets started.'

'That's true. They aren't children, though. Neither I nor anyone else can protect them for ever. They wouldn't want me to. No, I don't think I'm being unreasonable when I say that my responsibility ends with the provision of facilities – safeguarded facilities, mind – for my clients to get in touch with one another. What friendships they form then are strictly their own affairs. Have you anything to find wrong with that, inspector?'

Purbright realized that Mrs Staunch could be voluble when she liked. And she would like if he were to let himself sound critical. 'No,' he said smoothly, 'that sounds fair enough.'

Apparently mollified, she waited.

'As I understand it,' Purbright said after a while, 'you provided Miss Reckitt and later Mrs Bannister with a list each of gentlemen selected by you from your current clients as being potential matches for the ladies in question. Each list was in effect a set of descriptions, each description applying to a particular client and being accompanied by his code number. This number was the key to the man's name and address, known only to him and you. By the way, they're all three-figure numbers, aren't they?'

Mrs Staunch nodded. 'Even for the gentlemen, odd one's for the ladies.'

'Very well,' said Purbright. 'What you did not know, and cannot now tell me, is the identity of those clients who did in fact get in touch with Miss Reckitt and Mrs Bannister.'

'I'm afraid that is so.'

'Then have you a record of the lists which Miss Reckitt and Mrs Bannister received? You see what I am after – the names of men from whom these women had a choice. If a record exists, it would simplify my job tremendously.'

For the first time in the interview, Mrs Staunch looked bewildered.

'Record? No, I've no record of that kind. In any case, I can't compromise my clients. There's mutual trust involved here, inspector.'

'There may well be murder involved, Mrs Staunch.'

'We can't know for certain at the moment.'

'You must see the possibility, though. It's a rather more serious matter, surely, than professional etiquette.'

'That is too light a word, inspector, if you don't mind my saying so. My pledges to people who come here are not just points of etiquette.'

'No, I'm sorry. . . .'

She raised a hand and remained a moment in thought.

'I suppose,' she said, 'that in the circumstances you could be fairly insistent. You know – a search warrant or something?'

'I'd much rather that question didn't arise.'

After another pause she said: 'Look – as I told you, I've no record of those particular lists. But what I will do is this. I'll go through the file straight away, this evening, and try to reconstruct the one I sent Mrs Bannister. I know my own system and there's no reason why it shouldn't work out the same twice.'

'And Miss Reckitt?'

'No. That was too far back. Two months ago I tidied the files up quite a bit and a lot of the names won't be there any more.'

'Shall I send someone round in the morning?'

Mrs Staunch smiled. 'I'd rather you didn't, if you don't mind, inspector. I'll see that you get it as soon as possible.'

She showed him out by yet another of Handclasp House's many doors. This one led into a back lane. It was growing dark. A woman going by with a child glowered at him suspiciously.

Chapter Six

THE NEXT MORNING MRS STAUNCH CALLED AT THE POLICE
station and left a white foolscap envelope marked 'Highly
Confidential' which she requested the duty sergeant to place
immediately into the hands of Detective Inspector Purbright.

She then drove on through the town to Northgate and
parked her car against the railings of the Radical Club. She
saw, but paid no particular attention to, a trim and cheerful
looking woman of doubtful age who was gazing up towards
the building's balustraded roof. The woman held before her in
the manner of tourists and singers of hymns, an open book.
Yes, indeed, Miss Teatime was saying silently to herself, quite,
quite lovely. So it is.

Eventually Miss Teatime closed the book and ascended the
steps. She noticed the illuminated sign at the end of the hall,
knocked gently on the waiting-room door and entered. After
reading the two invitations, she responded to that on the left.

The room in which she found herself was subtly different
from the scene of Inspector Purbright's interview.

It was smaller and furnished in the style of a country parlour,
with flowery wallpaper, Welsh dresser and a pair of diminutive
armchairs that looked, in their loose covers, as if they were
curtseying beside the roughstone fireplace set with fir cones
on pink tissue paper. A copper warming pan gleamed on the
wall. Before a low, demurely curtained window, was an earthenware bowl containing hyacinths in bloom. Their perfume
drifted through the room where it became veined with the
smell of freshly unpacketed tobacco. It was while Miss Teatime
was delightedly savouring this combination that she noticed,
propped casually against the low brass fender, a pair of well
worn leather slippers.

Mrs Staunch entered. Over her costume and quite hiding

her jewellery was a fawn linen housecoat. She extended her hand.

'I am Sylvia Staunch.'

Miss Teatime looked very pleased to hear it. She grasped her bag and guidebook tightly and gave a little bob. Her smile came partly from good natured habit, partly from the sudden temptation to say Good morning, Mrs Tourniquet!

They sat facing each other in the armchairs.

'And do I take it,' opened Mrs Staunch in a creamy contralto, 'that you are thinking of joining our little circle?'

'Well,' said Miss Teatime, gazing at the slippers, 'I did happen to see your advertisement and I thought no harm would be done by coming along for a little talk.'

Mrs Staunch beamed. 'Exactly. Now just ask me whatever you would like to know.'

'I've only just arrived in Flaxborough, you see, and I think it is an altogether charming little town; I really do. Of course, London has been my home for many years, but I have not been fully happy there. . . .'

'The big city can be a very lonely place,' said Mrs Staunch.

'Indeed it can. And in recent years London has become so intimidating, somehow. The rushing about, the overcrowding . . . one simply has no time to stand and stare, as they say.'

'Are you a Londoner by birth, Miss . . .?' Mrs Staunch had already glanced at her prospective client's left hand.

'Teatime. Lucilla Teatime. No, as a matter of fact I was born in Lincolnshire. There are Teatimes in the Caistor area, you know. Perhaps that is why I had this urge to seek more rural surroundings. And I do like the sea, of course. Do you not find that Flaxborough smells of the sea?'

'We have a tidal river.'

'Tidal? Oh, how nice.'

'And there are the docks.'

'I am very fond of docks. Not,' she added dreamily, 'that I have ever been in one, you understand.'

Mrs Staunch thought the pun a trifle odd, but she smiled just the same.

'So now here you are in our little community and you feel you would like someone to share in the adventure. Is that how it is?'

'You could put it like that. A guide and comforter true,' twinkled Miss Teatime, 'is perhaps what I need.'

'No, seriously, I think you may have the right idea. I know how difficult it is to adapt to a new environment, and two heads are always better than one, are they not?'

'Well, not on the same neck,' replied Miss Teatime, biting her tongue just too late. She hastily added: 'As my uncle used to say. He was a bit of a card, the rector.'

'Of course,' Mrs Staunch went on, 'I think it is only fair to tell you that by no means everyone who comes here is accepted as a client. We are very selective. We insist upon two qualifications. A good background. And sincerity.'

'How wise you are,' agreed Miss Teatime.

'We do not ask for references. I flatter myself that I am a pretty sound judge of human nature and a personal impression is more valuable to me than any reference. That impression builds up from a dozen small points. Take the matter of fee, for instance. . . .'

'Yes, do,' said Miss Teatime.

'Take the matter of fee,' Mrs Staunch repeated firmly. 'Twenty guineas for a mere introduction may seem to some people a little high. But I know that a person of breeding, of integrity, has no difficulty in recognizing that a high fee is really designed for her protection – a sort of safety barrier against swindlers and' – a remark of Purbright's came back to her – 'and exploiters. It is also a test of sincerity. A true heart setting out to seek its fellow does not ask the cost of the journey.

You don't run cheap night flights, I suppose? Miss Teatime wanted to ask. Instead, she nodded gravely and took a peep into her handbag. Yes, the cheque book was there just behind a slim brown box.

Mrs Staunch rose and shifted a small mahogany table to Miss Teatime's chair. 'And now a spot of painless form filling,' she announced jocularly. 'It seems something we can't escape these days, doesn't it?' She went to a drawer in the Welsh dresser and returned with a foolscap sheet.

'Oh, dear, I'm terribly bad at forms,' lamented Miss Teatime. 'My stockbroker says I'll land myself in prison if I'm not careful.'

'Just you take your time, my dear. I've one or two things to see to in the office, so I'll leave you to it. Oh, by the way. . . .' Mrs Staunch bent and pointed to one of the questions on the form. 'This part about means is absolutely confidential, so don't worry. It's simply to give me a little guidance as to the sort of people you might like to meet.'

She left Miss Teatime nibbling her pen and looking as excited as a nun with dispensation to play Ludo.

A minute went by. Miss Teatime looked at the door and listened. Somewhere a typewriter was being tapped spasmodically. She glanced longingly down beside her at the handbag. No, she didn't want to shock poor Mrs Staunch. And yet. . . . An idea budded. She got up quickly and went to the window. It opened without trouble. Having carried to it the table and one of the chairs, she re-settled herself and lit the long, black cheroot she had taken from the box in her handbag. Then, carefully but with enormous relish, she expelled a stream of smoke through the open casement and began to write.

When Mrs Staunch returned, she noticed Miss Teatime's changed position and looked surprised.

'Please say you don't mind,' said Miss Teatime. 'I'm such a fresh air lover, and there did seem just a teeny touch of tobacco smoke in here when I arrived.'

'Of course I don't mind, my dear.'

'You don't think I'm an awful fuss-pot?'

'Not at all. Ah, we've finished our form filling, have we?'

Miss Teatime held it out shyly. 'I do hope it's all right.'

Briskly, Mrs Staunch read the form through. 'Fine,' she said at last. 'Just the ticket.'

'And just the cheque,' said Miss Teatime laughingly, handing it over.

Mrs Staunch sugared her careful scrutiny of the cheque by glancing again at the form and remarking: 'Isn't it a pretty name? Lucilla Edith Cavell Teatime. What a pity we have to introduce you simply as Miss 347!'

Simply, perhaps, but there came a quick result.

Miss Teatime was eating breakfast in the dining room of the Roebuck Hotel three mornings later when the receptionist brought to her table a white typewritten envelope. Inside was a smaller envelope addressed, in what Miss Teatime knew instinctively to be a firm masculine hand, to '347, c/o Handclasp Hall, Northgate, Flaxborough'.

She enjoyed the pleasant discipline of leaving the letter intact beside her plate until she finished her two sausages and scrambled eggs and eaten three pieces of toast and marmalade. Then she poured herself another cup of coffee and slit open the envelope.

The letter was quite short.

Dear Miss 347,

I wonder if you would like to write to me, as I understand you are interested in finding companionship. I, too, am a 'solitary soul' and would be very glad to hear from another such. Our ages, it seems, are about the same and I feel that we might have tastes in common. As I am in the happy position of not having to worry about earning a living (though not exactly one of the 'Idle Rich'!!) time does drag a bit so you will understand how hopeful I am of hearing from you.

Yours very sincerely,
4112 (R.N. retd.)

Miss Teatime read it through twice and was already framing a reply in her mind when she climbed, looking very pleased and determined, up the broad white staircase to her room.

She took a sheet of hotel notepaper from the letter rack beside the pot of cyclamen, then decided against it. No – no address at this stage. At the top of a piece of her own pale

sepia, deckle-edged stationery she wrote simply: c/o Handclasp House.

The rest of the letter flowed easily enough.

Dear Mr 4112,

I was so pleased to receive your letter this morning. It
had been forwarded to me very promptly and it gave me a
nice feeling of being less of a stranger in my new surroundings.

Now what can I tell you about myself?

I am unmarried (there, that is one thing you can put yourself at ease about!) and – like you, it seems – have no de-
mands on my time. This can be rather a bore, of course, but
I manage to keep myself occupied with walking (Nature is
a never-failing source of delight, don't you agree?); also
with trying my prentice-hand at writing (not much success
so far, alas!); and with dull, womanly things like needlework.

Perhaps I should mention one little weakness as well. I
have a passion – quite damaging to my bank account! – for
haunting antique shops. Flaxborough has already captured
me in this respect.

Do you like old things? They are a great reassurance, I
think, in this world of the tawdry and second-rate.

And of course, if you will forgive me for sounding terribly
unfeminine and practical, antiques are a marvellous investment.

Anything else? Oh, yes. You may smile, but I love the
sea! Of course, I couldn't help noticing that you are a Navy
man. But I must say nothing of my secret ambition or you
will think me silly and romantic and quite, quite unrealistic.

Sincerely yours,

347

Miss Teatime folded and put the sheet straight into its envelope. She never re-read her own letters before posting them.
Apart from having confidence born of long practice, she knew
that the embellishments and addenda that a second reading
might inspire would give the thing a calculated look. And that

would never do. Spontaneity, she reflected as she daintily
tongue-tipped the envelope flap, was everything.

She stayed in the bedroom long enough to finish the cheroot
she had lighted as an encouragement of literary invention.
Then she put on her coat and a hat, one of three bought the
previous day during what explorers and hunters would call a
gear collection and pocketed the letter. It would save time to
take it round herself. Anyway, it was a nice day for a walk and
she had noticed already how many attractive old inns there
were to be examined in Flaxborough.

An intinerary of a very different kind was being planned at that
moment by Inspector Purbright.

He had on the desk before him the list compiled by Mrs
Staunch. It was of five numbers, names and addresses, together
with such personal details of each nominee as apparently had
been considered relevant to his matrimonial prospects.

'Know anything about Joseph Capper, Sid?'

Sergeant Love, who had been standing looking out of the
window, suddenly swung round.

'Joe Capper, out at Borley Cross?'

'Aye. Home Farm.'

'Why, the crafty old bugger! He's got one already.'

'You mean he's married?'

'Has been for years. He lives in the farmhouse and she
shacks up in one of the outbuildings.'

'It sounds an amicable arrangement.'

'Oh, it's not arranged,' Love said. 'It's just that Joe happens
to be winning at the moment. Six months ago, it was the
woman who was in the house while Joe lived in the barn. They
think up tricks to get each other out. Sort of ding-dong siege.'

'Then what the hell is he doing with this marriage bureau
lark?'

Love shrugged. 'Trying to get reinforcements, I expect.'

The inspector read aloud from his list: '"312; Joseph
Capper, Home Farm, Borley Cross ... a stay-at-home but no
stick-in-the-mud, a man with acres and a mind of his own who

would share his home with a lady desirous of locking out her worries...." '

'Not half,' said the sergeant.

' "His hobbies are home-made wine and shooting...." '

'Is that the word it uses – *hobbies*?' Love looked incredulous.

'It is,' confirmed Purbright. 'Never mind, though; I can't see him being our man. I'll pay him a visit, just as a check, but whoever worked over Miss Reckitt and Mrs Bannister must have spent more time on it than Mr Capper is likely to have had to spare.

'Now then, who's next ...? 316; William C. Singleton, 14 Byron Road.... Do you know him?'

Love shook his head.

'He's a retired waterworks engineer, apparently. Good sense of humour ... handy about the house ... wants sympathetic woman to share beautiful garden....' Purbright looked up. 'You can have that one, Sid.'

The sergeant copied the address.

'Lot 324,' Purbright resumed. 'Plume, George; Prospect House, Beale Street....'

'You can cross *him* off.'

'Oh?'

'He's dead.'

'That does inhibit us a bit, doesn't it. How would he have ranked as a suspect, though?'

'The report of the funeral said he was ninety-four.'

It was Purbright's turn to register disbelief. He looked again at the Handclasp House prospectus. ' "... widower of three months, an active bee-keeper and tandem enthusiast, would welcome company of lively lady...." '

'That was George, all right,' said Love. 'A very well preserved old gentleman.'

Purbright put a valedictory pencil stroke through Mr Plume's paragraph, sighed and read on.

' "362; Leonard Henry Rusk, the Old Rectory, Kirkby Willows...." Rectory, Sid?'

The sergeant looked blank.

'The girl in the tea shop. You said she thought the man with Martha Reckitt looked like a clergyman.'

'She was a foreigner.'

'You don't find a rectory suggestive?'

'Not these days. All sorts of people live in them.'

'How about this, then – "while he awaits literary success he hopes to meet one who will fill a blank page in the book of life...."'

'Is all the stuff written like that?'

'I'm afraid it is. The standard argot of marriage bureaux, presumably. Mr Rusk is described as "reserved but with merry twinkle, owing his remarkable physical condition to a lifetime's devotion to sport". You can guess what that means.'

'Will you see him, or shall I?' Love added with careful gloom: 'It's a rotten bus service to Kirkby Willows.'

'All right. I'll go. You'll have to do this last one, though. Leicester Avenue. A bloke called Rowley, catalogue number 386. By the way, aren't they council houses in Leicester Avenue?'

Love confirmed that they were.

'He's a doubtful starter, then. Among the many things that con men and company directors have in common is fussiness about address.'

While Love made a second entry in his notebook, the inspector leaned back and made a final rapid survey of the list.

'I can't help feeling,' he said at last, 'that as a dispenser of hot tips Mrs Staunch leaves something to be desired. Incidentally, you do know what you're looking for, I suppose? Apart from samples of their handwriting.'

Love stood straight, staring a little way to his left. His boyish, bright pink face wore the slightest of frowns, like that of a carefully rehearsed pupil. With one hand he began to switch down the fingers of the other.

'A clever talker ...'

Purbright nodded.

'... who looks as if he might have a way with women.'

Another nod – and a gently lifted eyebrow.

'He's possibly got a sort of clergyman look about him. . . . Fair-haired – unless he's dyed it . . .'

The inspector's lips pouted commendingly.

'. . . and having facilities for hiding or geting rid of bodies.' This final qualification was produced with the air of a chairman hoping to surprise with the announcement of a bonus dividend.

Purbright gratifyingly slapped the edge of his desk. 'Bodies,' he repeated. 'Yes, indeed. It's their failure to turn up that's made this whole affair seem a bit unreal. If only we knew where these women used to meet the fellow, it might help. Our tree. . . .' he added, half to himself.

Love caught the remark.

'There are trees in Leicester Avenue,' he announced.

'Ah!' said the inspector, his eyes rounded.

He was a kindly man.

Chapter Seven

THE EYE BETWEEN THE WINDOW FRAME AND THE YELLOW, fly-mottled muslin was small and red and bright. It had a nervous, precise mobility. It was distrustful – hard as a little gun swivelling behind a fire slit.

'Anybody at home?' bellowed Purbright, knowing perfectly well that there was (an eye did not roll about a house on its own).

The muslin curtain was tweaked shut.

Purbright turned and leaned against the porch. He surveyed the yard, wondering in which of its surrounding buildings lurked the temporarily vanquished Mrs Capper. She could not have had a very wide choice: from one doorway came the booming of bullocks, from another the high argument of thirty or forty pigs, while chickens and turkeys contended for right of way in and out of a third. Perhaps there were upper storeys, though. Very useful to a good tactician....

He heard bolts being drawn and swung round to face the door again. There was a quickly widening gap. Then an arm shot out. In the next second he was stumbling into a big, dim room that smelled of bacon and paraffin. As the door thumped shut, something crashed against the outer step. It sounded very like a bottle.

'You should have come round to the other side, mister,' said a slow, faintly reproving voice. Purbright found it difficult to associate the voice with the piston-like arm that had whisked him into sanctuary. He looked at their owner's face and saw his old friend the eye, now revealed to have an associate.

'Now then,' said Mr Capper.

'Now then,' said Purbright amicably. He sat in the chair towards which Mr Capper had nodded and gazed round the room, taking his time. Country visitors, he knew, were fully

expected to go through this settling-in process before even
announcing their identity. In these more civilized parts, one
wasn't treated to a threshold frisking for information, as for
hidden weapons; it was for the caller to offer it when he
thought fit.

'I've just come over from Flax,' Purbright said.

'Oh, aye,' said Mr Capper.

'I'm a police inspector, actually. Purbright.'

'How do you do.'

'How do you do, Mr Capper.'

'Fair.'

'Barley looks well. That'll not leave you with much straw.'

'It's a new one, that. Supposed to be all head and no arse.'

'That's how you want it.'

'Aye.'

Joe Capper might well have been fed on his new barley. He,
too, had a large robust head, from which hair grew upwards
in spikes. A nicely ripened complexion considerably modified
the effect of the redness of his eyes. His body, though scarcely
stalk-like, was short and lean. He wore a heavy tweed jacket,
ancient, mudstained jodhpurs, and a pair of wellingtons so
many sizes too big that Purbright could have sworn that they
sent echoes of his conversation back up his legs.

'Like a drink?'

'I should,' said the inspector.

Mr Capper went to a wooden cupboard the size of a bus
shelter. Within its depths Purbright saw the window light reflected from the glazed bellies of half a dozen of the kind of
stone jar that in the country is called a grey hen. Joe carried
back to him a tumbler of honey-coloured liquid.

'Hollyhock,' he announced.

Purbright accepted the diagnosis without the least sign of
alarm. 'Cheers!' he said.

'All the best,' responded Mr Capper, going into a resolute
swig.

Purbright took a sip. A team of horses with white-hot hoofs
galloped down his throat.

'Very nice,' he said.

For a minute or two, a comfortable silence was maintained. Again Purbright let his gaze wander round the room. He was wondering how Mr Capper managed to go about his tasks on the farm without serious risk of the fortress falling in his absence.

He looked at the window and saw something he had not noticed before. To its catch was fastened a cord that ran upwards and over a hook in one of the ceiling beams. And suspended from this cord, revolving gently in a draught from the window, was a china vase of great size and tortuous design.

Mr Capper saw the direction his guest's interest had taken. 'Real heirloom, that is,' he said.

'Ah?'

'The wife's very fond of it.'

'I should think so.'

There was another pause, by no means uneasy. Purbright boldly tilted his glass and endured a second stampede of infernal stallions past his gullet. This time the after effects were quite pleasant; he felt capable and cunning.

'I wonder,' he said, 'if you know anything about jury service?'

'Not the first thing,' said Mr Capper.

Good, thought Purbright. 'The point is,' he went on, 'that you're down to be called to quarter sessions next week. I suppose that would be a bit awkward for you – as a farmer, I mean.'

'Bloody awkward.' Mr Capper glanced anxiously at the window and the pendant heirloom.

'In that case it might not be a bad idea for you to authorize your wife to take your place.'

'For me to *tell* her, do you mean?'

'Oh, no. We'd do the calling. All you need do is to give permission in writing. I'll take it now, if you like.'

In an instant the jubilant Mr Capper had produced a pad of cattle cake order forms and a pen. He turned one of the forms over and smoothed it flat.

'It'll be a nice little change for her,' he said to Purbright. 'Take her out of herself.'

'Just put: "I hereby authorize my wife" – then her full name – "to undertake jury service when so required". And sign it.'

'How do you spell authorize?'

Purbright told him. There were one or two more little difficulties. But the final document was legible and accurate enough.

One thing it most manifestly was not – a product of the same hand that had penned the three letters in Mrs Bannister's bedroom drawer.

'Mind you,' said Purbright, feeling some qualms as he pocketed the paper, 'it's not certain that your missus will be needed. I shouldn't say anything to her.'

'Oh, I'd not have done that anyway,' Mr Capper assured him. 'It'd spoil the surprise.'

After declining, with every show of regret, a second charge of his host's Hollyhock Holocaust, the inspector took his leave and departed by the recommended exit. Back doors, he reflected, could all too easily become a way of life.

The Old Rectory at Kirkby Willows was a tall, unattractive, late Victorian pile, set in a dank plantation of laurel and rhododendron. Several of the windows were uncurtained. One, on the upper floor, had been broken and masked with a sheet of hardboard. Purbright's use of the heavy ring knocker produced a hollow reverberation like an old man's cough. He had little hope of an answer.

Yet the door opened almost at once. He saw a man of perhaps thirty-five with a beard of that rather indeterminate kind that is generally vouchsafed to those who regard beard growing as a serious matter of policy. Henry Rusk also wore a dressing gown and the querulous expression of a disturbed creator. (Or so Purbright interpreted it.) His hair was light, almost blond.

Purbright announced his identity but not his business. That he had not yet decided himself. But policemen do not need to say why they have called. Nine householders out of ten are concerned at that stage only with getting them off the door-step; they would be just as hospitable towards a loud-voiced debt collector or a drunken auntie.

'We're just having tea,' said Henry Rusk, leading the inspector through a doorway on the left of the entrance lobby.

In the centre of an otherwise almost totally unfurnished room was a wooden kitchen table at which a woman was sitting. She was perhaps a little younger than Rusk, at whom she peered devotedly through a pair of black framed spectacles with thick lenses. Her black hair was straight and cut to the same length all the way round her head.

Rusk indicated her to Purbright.

'My mistress,' he said. 'She's called Janice.'

He resumed his seat at the table, leaving Purbright to dispose himself as he thought fit. The only alternative to standing proved to be a tea chest lying on its side in the big bay window.

As Purbright lowered himself on to that, he saw that Janice had before her a large brown loaf. At a nod from Henry she laboriously sawed off a slice which she handed over on the point of the knife. He buttered it while she watched.

'Shrimp,' Henry said, tersely.

Janice leaned forward, short-sightedly scrutinized a row of four or five little jars, then slid one across. Without acknow-ledgment, Henry picked it up and gouged out some of the contents. Janice neither ate nor drank anything herself.

The room was very cold. A smell of wet plaster pervaded it.

'And what are *you* after, then?' Henry spoke with his mouth full. He didn't look up from his plate.

Purbright resolved at that moment to be neither devious nor tactful. The tea chest was exceedingly uncomfortable.

'I understand you are a client of the Handclasp House matri-monial bureau.'

'I was,' replied Henry with neither hesitation nor, ap-parently, concern. 'But I got fixed up.'

Janice blushed happily.

'At first shot?' Purbright did his best to sound rude and was fairly successful.

'No.'

'How many?'

'I don't see what the hell it's got to do with you, but it so happens there were two others. One had been looking ten years for somebody to put her into a book. I put her on the next bloody bus. Then there was some bint who wanted to bear a beautiful child without taking her knickers off. God, this damn country's full of walking middle-class fantasies. It's got no loins any more.'

Henry glared at the loaf and Janice hastily began sawing it.

'Did either of your earlier, er, applicants happen to be called Reckitt?' Purbright asked. 'Or Bannister?'

'Tomato and pilchard,' said Henry, after brief consideration. Janice got busy among the jars.

'Names!' cried Henry, as soon as he had recharged his mouth. 'Why should I remember names? The only decent book written in the last fifty years hadn't a single name in it from cover to cover. This labelling obsession is a sign of literary castration. I'm a writer, man! A professional writer, not the compiler of a telephone directory.'

Henry's pronunciation of the word 'writer', Purbright noted, was the most aggressive instance of his general affection of a West Riding accent. He hurled forth the diphthong like the bleat of an agonized sheep.

'All the same, sir,' Purbright said, 'I should be glad if you would belabour your memory and see whether Reckitt or Bannister occurs to you.'

'Never heard of either of them. Who are they, anyway?'

'They are – or were – two of your fellow subscribers to that matrimonial agency. A Miss Martha Reckitt and a Mrs Bannister. Both women now appear to be missing.'

'Well I haven't lost them.' Henry passed a large white mug to Janice, who hastened to fill it with tea and hand it back. He tasted the tea, held it out for more sugar, then continued to take small sips while he read an item in the *New Statesman* that had been propped between his plate and a jar of jam.

'You say you are a professional writer?'

'That's right.' Henry didn't look up.

'In that case, perhaps you wouldn't mind obliging me with a sample.'

'What, of urine?'

Janice giggled admiringly.

'No, sir. I was thinking not so much in terms of original composition as of a simple specimen of handwriting. I'd settle for "The fox jumped over the lazy dog," for instance.'

'Or "The inquisitive copper vanished up his own arse-hole?"'

Purbright nodded blandly. 'That would do just as nicely, sir.' He strolled to the table, unscrewing the cap of his pen. The pen and a blank page torn from his notebook he placed beside Henry's elbow.

Henry stared at them. He looked less confident.

'What's the idea, anyway?'

'To use an old cliché, I am asking you to help us eliminate you from our inquiries.'

'You mean *I'm* suspected of something?'

'It does so happen that you bear some resemblance to a man who has been seen in the company of one of the women we're concerned about.'

'But that's bloody ridiculous.'

'You never associate with women?'

Henry screwed up his eyes in exasperation. 'Look, I'm a wri-i-iter, inspector. Of course I associate, as you call it. Connect up. Charge the battery. Absorb. I've got to feed my own parturition. Don't you see? It's like a furnace. No. No – a kiln. To get the white heat for beautiful porcelain, I've got to stoke, stoke, stoke it all the time. With people. All sorts of people. I don't have to be fussy like you, with your elimina-a-tions and your associa-a-tions. They just have to be real, and struggling, and smelling of the world's gut!'

There was a pause during which Purbright fancied he

could hear the word 'gut' echoing in the room's cold, huge-throated chimney. What he was afterwards to admit ashamedly to himself had been sheer malice provoked the observation that broke the silence.

'I think John Buchan's stuff is awfully good, don't you?'

With a choking noise, Henry Rusk seized the pen and held it poised. For fully a minute he gazed at the blank paper. Within the beard his mouth made fitful little movements. Then at last he groaned and began to write.

It was not until Purbright was well clear of the Old Rectory that he took one hand from the wheel, fished the paper out of his left hand pocket and glanced down to see what was on it.

The single line of writing was in a wavery, rather childish hand, not very easy to read.

It was: 'The fox jumped over the lazy dog.'

Chapter Eight

THERE CAME TO MISS TEATIME A SECOND LETTER BY THE SAME firm script as before, snug within its outer and inner envelopes and suggestive of dependable masculinity.

Again it was subscribed merely '4122 (R.N. retd.)' but its contents were more fulsome and, Miss Teatime dared to conclude, in warmer tone.

Dear Miss 347,

How can I describe my pleasure on receiving so prompt and friendly a reply to my little 'overture'. As it was my very first attempt through the agency, you can guess how 'chuffed' I was when it brought a result – your letter. People are not always very courteous in these selfish times and replies even to the sincerest inquiries cannot be relied upon. Still, you have proved that I do not need to despair altogether! Yes, as you have guessed, I am an 'old salt' (though not all that old, I assure you!) and of course I was thrilled to hear that you, too, have a love of the Deep. We must have talks about that when, as I am bold enough to hope, we meet.

So you are a writer (I could tell that from your letter, of course). You make me quite envious. Old shipmates have often told me that I ought to put my experiences into a book, but I never seem to have the time. Which is a pity, because a close friend of mine happens to be a very influential Literary Agent. He holds several publishers 'in the palm of his hand' and simply cannot get enough manuscripts – especially, he tells me, by women authors. We must see what *you* have hidden away there, mustn't we? And antiques – there's another coincidence! How I agree with what you say about 'this world of the tawdry and second-rate'. My

dear sister is always telling me that I spend too much of my
'humble sufficiency' on the works of old craftsmen, but she
does not understand the collector's 'mad joy in ancient
graven things and trinkets fondly wrought'.

Please tell me that we may meet. A word, a word, and all
will be arranged! !

So far, so jolly, jolly good, mused Miss Teatime, folding
the letter away in her handbag.

She looked at her little silver dress watch. Half past nine.
She decided against replying immediately to 4122. An impression of over eagerness would not be ladylike. Only a brief
note was needed this time; it could go tomorrow.

She crossed the corridor into the resident's lounge, collected the *Daily Mail* from a pile of papers on the central table,
and sank with it into a big grey chair. Flaxborough mornings
were very pleasant; nobody bothered one and there was
nothing of that sense imparted by London hotels of having to
keep one's feet tucked out of the way of anxious, self-important
people.

Reading a newspaper here was rather like casually scanning
dispatches from some mad, remote battlefield, so it was with
surprise and amusement that Miss Teatime spotted a Flaxborough dateline over a modest, down-page paragraph.

The story was nothing much – something about police inquiries into the disappearance of a local widow and the
possibility of connection with a previous, similar case – but
just to see the name Flaxborough in a national paper now had
a queerly personal significance.

An hour later Miss Teatime sauntered through the sunshine
to the public library, in whose almost deserted reference room
she added a few interesting snippets to what she knew about
Chippendale, Sheraton and Hepplewhite, besides finding time
for a quick cruise through *The Elements of Modern Seaman-
ship*.

It was just after midday when she left the library and made
her way along Church Street to the lane where she had dis-

covered, the day before, an altogether adorable inn.

This was The Saracen's Head, a thatched, whitewashed building so old that either the weight of its thick walls had caused it to sink during the centuries or the lane had risen by a succession of resurfacings. Through whichever cause, the pavement was now level with the tops of its windows. To reach the door, one had to descend a flight of five steps, each hollowed by wear into the semblance of a shallow tureen.

The bar room was long and dim and its air held the coolness of old stone. Lamps gleamed in the corners farthest from the window. Their soft yellow light – implying, one felt, a comfortable independence of time – was reflected from the black knuckles and sinews of oak furniture.

As Miss Teatime entered, the landlord rose from the company of his only three customers and stepped behind the bar. He was a big, sorrowful looking man whose Fair Isle pullover was rucked in wavelets from an unsuccessfully belted paunch. The quartet had been playing dominoes and the landlord clicked face down on the counter the hand of half a dozen pieces that had been nestling in his left palm. As soon as he had measured out her double whisky and her change, he retrieved the dominoes by pressing upon them the flat of his hand, and went back to the game.

Miss Teatime took a seat at a nearby table and for a while looked on with a benevolent eye. At the next interlude for the recharging of glasses, she rose and approached with modest hesitation.

'I wonder if I might sit and watch you for a while? I've always wanted to see how this game is played.'

There was a murmur of slightly embarrassed but respectful assent, and two of the players hutched along their bench to make room for her.

She sat primly beside a man in blue serge whose smile of assurance was somewhat marred by a cast in one eye. This gave the feeling of there being someone behind her shoulder and with whom the man was in confidential communication. However, as play progressed the conversation warmed again and

Miss Teatime soon found herself included.

She was impressed by the rapid calculation of which these people so obviously were capable. Their power of divination was perhaps even more remarkable. But most of all she marvelled at the way each could hold ten, twelve, fourteen 'cards' in one perfectly secure palmful.

Two more games had been played and fresh drinks brought in. The ivory tablets swirled and rattled in another shuffle. Hands reached out to divide them.

'I wonder,' quickly said Miss Teatime, 'if I . . . .'

They looked at her.

'What I mean is, would it spoil your game terribly if I had a go? I think I can see how it's played.'

There was a moment's silence. The landlord glanced at the others. 'All right,' he said. 'You have a try, duck.' He slid a helping of cards towards her.

Happily, Miss Teatime began to pick them up and to build a little crescent shaped wall. 'I haven't quite such big hands as you gentlemen,' she explained.

'You just suit yourself, pet,' the cast-eyed man told her. 'I'll not look at them.' Oddly enough, that appeared to be exactly what he *was* doing at that moment, but Miss Teatime had been too well brought up to view uncharitably the afflictions of others.

'Right, then,' said the landlord. 'Your drop, Jack.'

'Oh, there is one thing,' Miss Teatime announced, 'that I really must insist upon.' She gave a nervous smile. 'There can be no question of my not "taking my corner", as I think you describe it. Pints – that's right, isn't it? And if I *should* win . . . oh, but that's hardly likely!'

'Whisky it'll be if you do,' gallantly asserted the landlord.

Miss Teatime blushed. 'But just a single. Naturally.'

The play began.

Two hours later, when the irrefutable fact of closing time (The Saracen's Head not being, after all, in another world) lay heavy upon the rest of the company, Miss Teatime was brighter than they by nine glasses of spirits. The mastery of dominoes, like that of anything else, simply called for a certain knack. She was pleased, but not arrogant at her success in having discovered it among her reserve talents.

The landlord climbed ponderously to his feet, stretched, and stood looming over them.

'Glasses, if you please,' he intoned.

'It's not time yet,' said the man called Jack.

Miss Teatime smiled mischievously into her tenth glass of whisky. 'Old crusty crutch!' she said. Jack laughed and nudged her.

'It's three o'clock,' affirmed the landlord.

Miss Teatime ostentatiously consulted her dress watch. 'Two minutes to,' she corrected.

The man with the odd vision stared at a vase of flowers in the window in order to see the clock on the wall of a building across the street. 'That's right,' he said. 'Two minutes to go yet.' He turned and the landlord received, by proxy, as it were, the gaze of admiration intended for Miss Teatime.

'He's mean with his bloody minutes, is old Fred,' declared the third customer. Jack noisily concurred and nudged Miss Teatime again.

She grinned, then suddenly adopted an expression of prim disapproval.

'My considered opinion of old Fred,' she said carefully, 'is that he would twist the skin off a fart.'

In the C.I.D. room at Flaxborough Police Station, Inspector Purbright and his sergeant conferred. Neither felt that he had gathered anything useful, but the fleeting appearance, ten minutes before, of the Chief Constable in the doorway with his 'Found those ladies yet?' could not be ignored. He had looked a bit like the ghost of Hamlet's father.

'I'll bet Spain's been on to him,' Purbright said. 'It's from Spain that he gets the meat for those tree rats of his.'

Love, who had been twice bitten by Mr Chubb's Yorkshire terriers, agreed. Any man who would knowingly supply pro-

vender for such creatures was quite capable of putting pressure
on a chief constable.

Purbright glanced through the file, which now combined
what information they had about both Miss Reckitt and Mrs
Bannister. There were also five specimens of handwriting,
none of which bore close resemblance to the three 'Rex' letters,
although the experts had expressed tantalizing doubts about
Mr Rusk's O's and the T-crossing of Mr Rowley of Leicester
Avenue.

'I'd like it to be Rusk,' Purbright admitted, 'but I'm quite
sure he's in the clear. For one thing, the impersonation of
charm is unquestionably beyond him. For another, he's far
too convinced of his literary professionalism to be able to pretend that he is a successful author, as women like Mrs Bannister would understand the term. Mr Rusk might invent a
literary luncheon, but he most certainly would not invent the
presence at it of J. B. Priestley.'

'You don't think Rusk is a fraud, then?'

'My dear Sid, of course he's a fraud. But not the kind we are
looking for. It takes more than a fringe of whisker and some
bowelly borrowings from D. H. Lawrence to make a real im-
postor – even if you chuck in the stage Yorkshire as well.
There's a sort of splendour about the phoneyness of a con
man. It's an apparatus that he's spent years in building up and
perfecting – an elaborate fair organ. Mr Rusk couldn't whittle
a wooden flute.'

'When you put it like that,' said Love after an admiring
pause, 'I'm afraid my two blokes are out, too.'

'Rowley and. . . .' Purbright turned back through his notes.

'And Singleton. The retired waterworks man.'

'That's right. How did you get on?'

'Well, they didn't seem very pleased to see me. Singleton
wouldn't come out of the garden. He was going up and down
with a lawn mower all the time. I had to ask each question as
he went by one way, and try and catch the answer when he
passed on the way back.'

'Very trying for you, Sid.'

'Not really. The answers were all very short. And him being so busy made it easier to get the writing samples. I just pinched three or four of the labels off his rose bushes. Of course,' Love added, nodding at the file, 'I trimmed them down a bit and mounted them properly.'

'So I noticed. Most neat. Now I understand why I couldn't make much sense out of "Peace Mrs Pettifer Brevitt's Pride Lancashire Ascending".'

'He denied that he'd met anybody at all up to now through that matrimonial thing. There's one lady he's writing to after dark, but he's not actually fixed anything up yet.'

'After dark?'

'When he can't see any longer in the garden.'

'Oh.'

'I honestly don't think Singleton can have done anybody.'

'It doesn't sound like it. What about Rowley, then? I gather he didn't strike you as villain material either.'

The sergeant shook his head. 'I think he's a little bit simple. He goes in for competitions. Hundreds of them. There were papers all over his front room with bits cut out. Actually, he thought I'd come to tell him he'd won some tomato soup thing that would give him a holiday for four in the West Indies or somewhere. As soon as he answered the door, he dashed back inside and brought me three empty tins and said "Vigo Vegetables for Vigour". I felt a proper twat.'

'You disabused him, of course?'

'Well, not straight away, actually. I remembered what you'd said about being tactful.'

Purbright regarded him sternly. 'Tact should not be confused with mendacity, sergeant.'

'Mendacity?'

'Telling lies.'

Love looked relieved. 'Oh, I didn't tell him any lies. I just said that I was very sorry but I didn't seem able to put my hand on the Why-I-Always-Use-Vigo-Soup slogan that he'd submitted and could he let me have a copy.'

Purbright's expression did not relax.

'Well,' Love added, 'it did seem an opportunity for using initiative.'

'How did you know about the slogan?'

'I . . . I guessed.'

The inspector gave him a shrewd stare, then looked down at the file. He read out with measured gravity: ' "I go with Vigo because Vigo Soups are the Stuff for the Troops".'

His gaze was upon the sergeant's face once more. 'I do hope,' he said, 'that *your* entry was a bit better than that.'

If Love blushed, the effect upon his normally rubicund complexion was not apparent.

'I shall have to see Mrs Staunch again,' Purbright announced. 'I don't know how many clients she has, but it looks as if we shall just have to work through the lot.'

'Couldn't it be someone who's just using the agency as a blind?' suggested Love, anxious to rehabilitate himself.

'How do you mean, Sid?'

'Well, you said there are records of all these people like Mrs Bannister and so on in the office there. I don't expect the place is all that difficult to get into. Suppose somebody did that and jotted down a few names and then wrote to them afterwards. I mean, he wouldn't need to become a customer himself, would he?'

Purbright considered.

'You have a point. Breaking in would be simple enough – and it wouldn't have to be obvious, either. The trouble is that in the first instance the letters have to be addressed by number for forwarding.'

'He'd have the numbers, though. He'd send a letter to the agency and Mrs Whatsername would forward it on. She'd not know anything was wrong.'

'True. What about the victim's reply, though? He couldn't go and collect it.'

'He wouldn't have to. Not if he'd put his address at the top of his own letter and asked the woman to write back to him direct.'

The inspector remained silent. The argument was not helpful, but it was certainly tenable. He reached for the telephone directory.

'Consider yourself redeemed, Sid. You might have got something.'

With the expression of a rewarded retriever, Love watched Purbright dial and dispatch introductory civilities to Mrs Staunch. After a while he heard him come to the point.

'Look, something has just crossed my mind – or rather it's been led across it by my very perceptive sergeant – which could have some bearing on the matter we discussed the other day.... That's right – the two ladies we're looking for. What I'd like you to do is to think back carefully and see if you can remember anything to suggest someone's having got into your office – you know, broken in or sneaked in – while you weren't there.... Yes, in the last couple of months or so....'

He hunched the phone between shoulder and ear while he lit a cigarette. Love heard the undulating squeak of whatever Mrs Staunch was saying.

Purbright spoke. 'One of the windows.... Yes, I know – over the lane at the back.... Nothing actually stolen, though.... No, I see.... No.... Anyway, I'm much obliged to you.... Well, it may and it may not – probably not, actually. Thanks all the same. Oh, just one other thing. I'm afraid I'm going to have to take a look for myself at those files of yours. It really can't be helped.... Tomorrow, probably.... Fine, yes. I look forward to seeing you again.'

Thoughtfully he replaced the receiver.

'She thinks she had a burglar, as she puts it, not very long after Christmas. She can't remember exactly. It was during cold weather, though, because that is why she particularly noticed that this window at the back had been left open slightly. Nothing was missing, as far as she knows, but she did get the impression that the stuff in the filing cabinet had been rummaged a bit.'

'There you are, then,' said Love.

'Oh, yes. Here we are, indeed. But you can see what dismal prospect this opens up. Instead of a few dozen suspects, nicely docketed with addresses provided, we now have the entire male population to choose from.'

Love swallowed and glanced down at his shoes. He looked like a man who has flicked away a cherry stone and derailed an express.

'Never mind,' Purbright told him. 'It may be simpler to go about things in a different way. The opposite way, actually. So far, we've worked on the assumption that the man we want must be one of those who have registered with the agency. We can't assume that any more. But unless we can find him by another means — and remember that we don't know the first thing about his appearance or movements or where he lives — all we can do is wait for him to go into operation again.'

'What, kill another woman!'

'Of course not. In any case, we don't know yet that anybody's been killed; he may be just laying in a harem, like some of those farmers down on the marsh. No, what I mean is that if we stop chasing round after the hunter and keep watch on the quarry instead, we'll probably stand a much better chance of nabbing him.'

'You think he'll have another go, then?'

'Unless he's moved on, yes. There invariably enters an element of habit into these things, Sid. And it isn't as if the profits so far have justified retirement. Four hundred pounds doesn't last long these days, and I can't see that Miss Reckitt would have had much in the way of realizable assets.'

'I feel sorry for them,' said Love, firmly. It sounded as though he had just made up his mind about something slightly embarrassing.

Purbright gave a slow, thoughtful nod. 'So do I. Very sorry. Not because they were robbed. Or murdered, even. It's the insult that must have really hurt.'

Chapter Nine

MRS STAUNCH MET THE INSPECTOR WITH AN EXPRESSION OF repressed excitement and annoyance. Without a word, she admitted him to her office and went straight to the window.

'Now, then – what do you think of that?'

She pointed to the small gap between the sill and the bottom of the frame. Purbright saw marks on the woodwork that suggested the insertion of a screwdriver or chisel. They were fresh marks.

He raised his brows. 'Last night?'

'And to think it was just yesterday afternoon that you rang up and I told you about that other time. I don't know *what* to think, really!'

'It is odd, isn't it?' Purbright agreed. He peered at the marks, then examined the rest of the window. The catch was old and loose; it would have slipped off with very little persuasion.

'Anything missing?'

'They've been in *there* again.' Mrs Staunch indicated the filing cabinet.

Purbright took out his handkerchief and eased forward the top drawer. Its contents did seem less tidy than when he had glanced at them on his previous visit.

The significance of the handkerchief was not lost on Mrs Staunch. 'I'm afraid I can't say that I haven't touched anything, inspector. I didn't notice the window straight away.'

'No, I shouldn't have expected you to. It would be as well, though, if we observe the Agatha Christie rules from now on. I'll get someone over.' He reached for the telephone. 'May I?'

In less than ten minutes there arrived Detective Constable Harper, bearing a leather case and a camera the size of a hurdy-gurdy.

The outing was clearly a treat for him. He loped around the little room like an exploring Gibbon and happily spooned great quantities of grey powder on all accessible surfaces, including several that took account of the possibility of the intruder's having been eight feet tall.

'He won't hurt anything, you know,' Purbright said to Mrs Staunch in a murmured aside. She did not appear convinced.

'No – those are very private,' she called. Harper had been in the act of lifting some of the folders out of the filing cabinet. He looked inquiringly at Purbright.

'Just the covers, Mr Harper ... no, on second thoughts, you'd better leave them alone altogether. If he wore gloves, you'll be wasting your time, and if he didn't, there'll be better prints on what you've got already.'

Mrs Staunch gave him a small smile of gratitude.

From that point, Harper's inspiration rapidly evaporated and soon he was dismantling his props and packing lenses and bottles and plates and brushes back in their compartments of the leather case.

'It's quite a business, isn't it?' observed Mrs Staunch, rather nervily. The worst part of the ordeal, although she did not say so, had been Harper's habit of continuously whistling one tune – the March of the Toreadors – through closed teeth while he worked.

Almost immediately after his departure, a buzzer sounded. Mrs Staunch glanced up at an indicator on the wall. One of its pair of electric bulbs flickered for several seconds.

'I'm afraid a client has just come in,' she explained. 'Would you mind if I left you now, inspector?'

'Not in the least,' Purbright assured her. 'I shall be busy myself for a little while.' He patted the cabinet in explanation.

Mrs Staunch hesitated, frowning. Then she shrugged and opened the door. 'You will remember what I said, won't you? About confidences? I mean, they're the whole essence. . . .' She left the sentence unfinished, but there was a plea in her eyes.

'Of course, Mrs Staunch. I really do understand.'

The door closed.

Purbright soon found that what the proprietress would have called her 'ladies' section' was less crowded than the reference numbers – three hundred and upwards – suggested. The system was doubtless based on the same psychological principle as that employed by newspapers to make the volume of box advertising seem bigger than it really was.

The number of recent registrations – and only in these was he interested – was about a dozen. He removed them from the file and read them through carefully.

Nearly all told the same story, though it had to be reached through a terminology of cheerful cliché which had been obviously adopted at Mrs Staunch's dictation. It was an ordinary, if saddening, tale of women whose lack of youth, money and social graces threatened a lonely and comfortless future. Purbright suspected that most of the applicants could have ill afforded the twenty guinea fee. Three, he noticed, were old age pensioners; two others, the widows of farm labourers. A sixth, who hopefully offered 'careful housekeeping and good cooking in home of suitable gentleman', was a school canteen helper. Under 'Means (for office use only)', one woman had written: 'Maintenance money, four pounds per week'.

Not exactly a rich field, Purbright reflected, for criminal exploitation.

There were two forms, however, whose promises were distinctly above average.

The first of these had been filled in by a woman called Rose Prentice, age 58, divorcée. Her occupation was described as stock breeding and farm management; her hobbies, not unexpectedly, as riding, shooting and dog showing. She had written in the Personal Appearance section simply 'Good seat' and through 'Means' had dashed a short, heavy line. Purbright did not doubt that this was an intimation of land ownership and the firm resolve to hang on to it.

The qualities for which Mrs Prentice looked in a mate were expressed with equal bluntness. He would have to be strong, energetic, used to stud work and willing to muck out. A tolerance of children would not come amiss: the farm was always being visited by one batch or another of the many grand-children in the family.

Purbright made the experiment of thinking of himself as a confidence man and of Mrs Prentice as his victim. Rose, I love you, how about making the farm deeds over to me. I'm awfully good at managing things – *Have you done the mucking out yet?* – Not yet, could I have five hundred pounds for that tractor I told you about which is such a bargain? – *We've a tractor already, if you're really hard up there's three and six egg money in the cash box in the bread pippin* – Please let me handle your insurance, dear Rose, and I will devour you with kisses – *Here's my card and this week's stamp; now then, are you used to stud work?* – What with twenty-seven kids hanging about? You're jo....

Purbright started, as if from a dream that had begun to lead him down sinister by-ways. He shut the folder and added it to the rejects.

One candidate remained. A second perusal of her form left the inspector in no doubt of his having discovered an almost perfect bait. He quickly copied the details into his notebook, then put all the folders away in their proper order in the drawer.

Before finally closing it, he made a rapid scrutiny of the record of Mrs Staunch's male clients, but found none that seemed any more worthy of close investigation than the five on whom time had been wasted already.

Quietly he let himself out of the back door.

Sergeant Love greeted the name of Purbright's find with sceptical amusement.

'Lucilla Edith Cavell Teatime ... oh, cripes! No wonder she wants to change it.'

'At least it's memorable. That should help you a bit, Sid.'

'Me?'

'Yes. You are hereby assigned to her. If she were a mere Miss Smith or Miss Jones, you might forget whom you were supposed to be following, or at least grow lax in observation.

But let me tell you about Miss Teatime.

'She admits to being forty-three years old, but her middle names suggest birth during the first world war, so fifty is probably nearer the mark. What she looks like you will have to find out for yourself. She is staying at the Roebuck, so Jim Maddox might be helpful to you. Or there's that tottie who used to fancy you – the one in the tap. . . .'

'Phyllis Blow?' Love looked alarmed.

'Oh, I don't know her name,' Purbright said in a way that implied fornication to be a triviality with which those above the rank of sergeant were not concerned. 'Anyway, how you get in tow in the first place is up to you; what I want is a report of where the Teatime goes and – more important – whom she meets. Do you think you can do that?'

'I don't see why not,' said Love. 'She can't trot round much if she's all that old.'

'What do you mean – all *that* old?'

'You said you thought she was fifty.'

Purbright turned upwards an expression of pious resignation. 'Yes, Sid. But might I offer a word of advice? Don't assume that extreme old age necessarily brings deafness and failing eyesight. I'm asking you to follow this woman unobtrusively – not like a porter in a geriatric ward.'

'She'll not spot *me*,' declared Love, unabashed.

He thought a moment.

'But why do we *have* to follow her? Can't you sort of confide in her and get her to let us know what happens? I mean, it would save a lot of . . .' he nearly said 'buggering about' '. . . duplication.'

Purbright shook his head. 'She's probably a pretty timid soul, remember. We couldn't say anything to her without letting on that it might be a crook she's going to meet. Even if she agreed to help, she'd be too nervous to be of any use.'

The sergeant acknowledged the logic of this and set off at once for the Roebuck Hotel.

The manager, Mr Maddox, said he would be only too

happy to assist in any way he could. He did hope, however, that Miss Teatime (who had impressed him as being a very respectable lady) was not, ah, not in any way, er. . . .

No, said Love, she wasn't. He had been told to keep an eye on her purely for her own good – that was all.

Mr Maddox was glad to hear it. One could so easily be deceived in people: one minute they were slipping sixpences into the blind stocking at the cocktail bar, the next they might be burning lavatory seats in a bedroom grate.

Love expressed awed appreciation of this hazard and asked if Miss Teatime was available at that time to be covertly observed

Mr Maddox regretted that she was not; she had gone out, as was her morning custom. However, if the sergeant would come into the dining room and take lunch at one o'clock or thereabouts, he, Mr Maddox, would make a point of identifying her.

Love saw that his assignment promised to be a higher class and more elastic business than his usual routine of taking stolen property lists round the second hand shops, interviewing youths suspected of smashing wash basins at the Assembly Rooms and asking to produce their dog licences such of Mr Chubb's neighbours whose pets happened to have fallen foul of his marauding Yorkshire terriers. Accordingly, he spent the next hour in the Roebuck Tap, on the other side of the yard, where two halves of bitter and as prolonged a view as he dared take of Miss Phyllis Blow's mammary canyon left him feeling quite pleasantly raffish.

At ten past one, he wandered into the dining room. Mr Maddox was standing at the huge sideboard, mixing a salad dressing. He gave Love a knowing smile over the vinegar bottle and nodded to signify that the lady of whom he wotted was present already.

With the defensive instinct of those who rarely eat in restaurants, Love selected a table against the wall farthest from the door. He drew from his pocket the newspaper that he had remembered to buy especially for the occasion and bivouacked behind it.

Only half a dozen tables were occupied. He peeped over the top of the paper at each in turn. That, he decided, must be Miss Teatime – a woman sitting alone to whom a waitress was carrying soup.

The woman turned and smiled at the waitress. She looked rather pleasant, Love thought – almost attractive. No chicken, though; there was quite a bit of grey in her hair. Her pale blue costume, while not 'gear', was smart and she sat with the straight-backed dignity that Love tended to associate with aunts, librarians and other strictly a-sexual characters. It was a pity that she seemed so well preserved. Healthy women of that generation were confoundly keen on walking as a rule. Love's toes curled apprehensively.

It was Mr Maddox who came to take his order.

'The lady in blue, on her own,' he whispered to the menu.

'That's what I thought,' said Love.

'I take it you don't want her to know that you're ... you know – bodyguarding?'

'Good lord, no!' Love breathed. 'Braised steak,' he said aloud.

'Mum's the word,' the manager hoarsely assured him, then 'Soup, sir?' he boomed.

'No soup.' Love remembered that his quarry was one course ahead.

He hid behind his paper again and observed the delicate raising and lowering of Miss Teatime's spoon. Her head was held gracefully, just a fraction forward, and had none of that curious motion – half butt, half scoop – that most soup drinkers find it necessary to adopt. She held the spoon at the very end of its handle and gave it the appropriate lateral twist with her wrist but with fine flexible fingers. Love found himself wondering if his young lady would prove amenable to instruction along similar lines; the effect really was dinky.

Thus preoccupied, the sergeant did not notice that Mr Maddox, having passed his order to the second waitress, was now stooped in guarded talk with another favoured customer. This was George Lintz, editor of the *Flaxborough Citizen*, a wiry man with a lean, mistrustful face bisected by a wide, apparently lipless mouth.

The manager was not actually imparting information. He repeated nothing of what Love had said. But he was a man within whom confidences lay like heavy, indigestible suppers. He would have burst if denied the relief of passing, with sidelong glances and tucked-in chin, gusts of portentous innuendo. No great harm was done. All Mr Lintz gathered was that if everything were told about middle-aged ladies in blue costumes, an eye or two might be opened ... that an hotel manager could write a book if so minded ... that it took all sorts, and that, in a word, one never knew.

The editor, who was accustomed to this sort of importuning, bore it philosophically and forgot it as soon as Mr Maddox had sidled away.

There was someone else, however, who did not forget.

Miss Teatime had caught nothing of what the manager had been saying. But she did notice, without appearing to look in that direction, that some of Mr Maddox's accompanying gestures were towards herself.

One didn't mind being talked about, of course; it was nicer than being ignored all the time. The interesting thing was *why* one had been chosen as a topic.

Miss Teatime put down her soup spoon and looked around with an air of leisurely innocence. She gave an answering smile to one of the waitresses and to an elderly gentleman at another table. What she was really seeking was a sight of the person with whom the manager had been talking before he passed on to that rather common looking man with the thin mouth.

Just then, the waitress arrived at Love's table with his braised steak. He lowered his newspaper, beamed at her, and pressed himself back into his chair while she arranged dishes.

Miss Teatime took the opportunity of scrutinizing him as thoroughly as a distance of twenty feet allowed.

She decided that he was young, florid, capable within certain rather narrow limits, persistent and basically good natured. Quite likeable, in fact ...

Miss Teatime looked away again and mentally added the qualification:

... for a policeman.

Chapter Ten

ALTHOUGH SERGEANT LOVE HAD BEEN BORN AND BRED IN FLAX-
borough and gravitated there once again after a few years'
service in other police divisions, he would not have claimed
exhaustive knowledge of the town. Natives of any place have
a tendency to take for granted those areas and features that
lie outside the immediate orbit of home and work. Policing, of
course, did make that orbit much wider in his case. Even so,
there were lanes he had never entered, closes he had never
explored, riverside walks that never had known his reluctant
feet.

Miss Teatime was to be the instrument of the filling in of
nearly all those gaps.

It seemed at first that she was a slow walker, much given
to halting for the contemplation of such things as coping
stones and door posts and coal hole covers and old fashioned
street lamps. But Love soon learned how remorselessly she
could clock on the mileage without any apparent effort. He had
only to take his eyes off her slim, upright back for a few
moments to find, on glancing again in her direction, that she
had moved on and was rounding a corner a hundred yards
away.

She led him, for two foot-stewing, thigh-racking days, past
practically every name in the Flaxborough street directory and
into parts of the outskirts that might, to his eyes, have been
precincts of Kiev or Medicine Hat.

He slogged along wharves, banged his head in a tunnel
under Barnet Street and trailed up a steep lane that led to
what seemed to be a ruined keep. During other excursions, he
found himself, for the very first time in his life, in the Grainger
Museum and Art Gallery, a permanent exhibition of folk
crafts in an annexe of the public library, and (very briefly) a

ladies' convenience in Brown and Derehams.

On the third day, the sergeant rested. But the circumstances were of Miss Teatime's devising, not his own.

He had risen early and taken up his post in the diminutive room which Mr Maddox had put at his disposal and which commanded views of the hotel staircase and the doors of dining room and lounge. He could glimpse, just inside the dining room, Miss Teatime eating her breakfast.

Miss Teatime could not see the sergeant, but she guessed he was not far away; for forty-eight hours his face had bobbed in remote corners of her excellent vision like a pink lantern left burning in daylight. She was not unduly concerned, merely a little curious. And as she spread marmalade and began to read the letter lying by her plate, the thought of her rosy visaged familiar was for the moment dispelled altogether.

'4122 (R.N. retd.)' expressed delight at her having agreed to a meeting and would 'weigh anchor' that very day in response to the signal he had so keenly awaited. Would she be in the Garden of Remembrance by St Laurence's Church at eleven bells precisely....

At this point, Miss Teatime paused. She had a vague idea that 'bells' meant something different from the hours of ordinary land-based folk. But no, he would not expect her to work such things out; it doubtless was just another of his jocular figures of speech.

She read on.

I am sure I shall recognize you on instinct (do you believe in Telepathy?) but just to make sure that neither of us accosts some perfect stranger (! !) I suggest you take the seat nearest the water fountain and have in your hand some flower or piece of greenery. You will spot me, I expect, by my ugly old quarter-deck mug! (No, I am joking – my face is not all that fearsome really) ...

Quarter-deck, Miss Teatime repeated to herself. Did they *have* quarter-decks these days? Perhaps they did....

I am most intrigued by this 'Secret Ambition' that you mention. Are you not going to tell me what it is? I promise faithfully not to think you 'silly and romantic'. In any case, aren't we all, at heart?

Forgive me if I write no more just now, as I have to board a train for the Big City – a rare thing these days, thank goodness, but time and tide and directors' meetings wait for no man, I'm afraid!

Until we meet,

Yours impatiently,

4122 (It's Jack to my friends, if you'd like to know!)

Miss Teatime folded the letter and thoughtfully stirred her coffee. Today was going to be one occasion when the pleasant young policeman would have to be deprived of a passage in her wake....

She smiled at the way the phrase had popped into her head: maritime metaphor seemed to be infectious.

Ten minutes later, Love watched Miss Teatime emerge from the dining room and disappear from his view at the first turn of the stairs. He was not sorry that she apparently intended to go straight out this morning, relinquishing her usual hour of reading the papers in the lounge. His hideout – actually an empty store cupboard with a small glass panel high in the door – was stuffy and uncomfortable.

Another quarter of an hour went by. Love dutifully kept his face pressed to his tiny window.

Nearly half an hour. He propped the door a couple of inches open and breathed in the air from the corridor. It smelled of cooking vegetables.

The clink of distant glasses told him that the bars had opened.

The cupboard had become unbearable. He stepped stiffly into the corridor and took a few cautious turns up and down.

After a while, this, too, palled. Love went out into the street. He crossed over and found a shop doorway in which he could enjoy the morning sunshine and keep an eye on the pillared entrance of the Roebuck at the same time.

A fair number of people greeted him as they passed. Several stopped and showed readiness to chat. The detective 'tails' on films and television, Love ruefully reflected, didn't have *their* job complicated by acquaintance with so many friendly and garrulous citizens; nobody as much as glanced at them.

Eventually, an increasing suspicion that he had blundered in some way made the small talk and disrespectful banter of the strolling Flaxborovians insupportable. He went back to the hotel and sought the advice of Mr Maddox.

Another way out of the building? Well, there was and there wasn't, said Mr Maddox enigmatically. But before he considered the point more closely, perhaps it would be wise to establish whether Miss Teatime were still in her room. He sent a chambermaid to find out, enjoining tact with such gravity that the girl immediately assumed a scene of vicious abandonment to be in store and so took a friend from the kitchen to share.

Both were disappointed.

'Not there,' said Mr Maddox. 'Ah. In that case, she must have gone down the service stairway at the back, which guests never do. I must say, I'm surprised. But it just goes to show.'

He spread his hands and went off to supervise the setting of tables.

Love gloomily repaired to the Tap to await lunch time and the possible reappearance then of 'the subject' (from the remembered terminology of espionage he picked the word with sour annoyance).

Phyllis was behind the bar. But this time she was wearing a sombre woollen dress buttoned right up to her chin.

Everybody was being rotten to him today.

The Garden of Remembrance was a hedged enclosure won from the older part of St Laurence's cemetery through the efforts of a particularly Toc H-minded vicar. It was nearly square and the gravel paths round its perimeter and across the diagonals gave it the semblance of a flag, with a domed drinking fountain as its central motif.

There were two teak seats on each of the four sides and four more seats were grouped round the fountain. The geometrically spaced flower beds contained geometrically arranged plants. Every plant of the same species was of identical size and seemed even to bear a precisely similar number of leaves and flowers. At each corner and in the centre of each side was a Lombardy poplar. Exactly between them, cypresses had been set. The trees were young, but already they helped the privet hedge to shelter the garden from winds and to make traffic noise seem farther off.

Miss Teatime opened the low, wrought iron gate into the garden at five minutes to eleven.

Several women, two with prams, were settled in seats round the sides. A group of three old men sat together, gazing resignedly straight ahead. They wore long black coats and their cloth caps were tilted forward almost to their eyebrows. Two children raced up and down the diagonal paths and chased each other round the drinking fountain. Eventually one of them fell over and was carried back to a seat by his mother, who made noises even more unnerving than his and who seemed incensed not by his late boisterousness but by his imperfect mastery of balance.

There was no one in the garden who looked likely ever to have walked a quarter-deck.

Miss Teatime strolled to the centre of the square, remembering the injunction to choose the seat nearest the fountain. To her eye, though, all four looked equidistant, so she picked the one that gave the easiest view of the entrance.

Then she realized that she had not provided herself with the requested flower. Would it really matter? There was no one else in this part of the garden with whom she might be confused. On the other hand, her correspondent did seem a rather particular man – seafaring, she had heard, tended to make one a stickler for detail. It might be as well to conform.

Cautiously, she slid her right arm down between the slats

of the seat behind her and found she could just touch the soil of the flower bed. Her hand moved from side to side in search of vegetation. It brushed a leaf. By stretching to the limit she managed to close finger and thumb upon a couple of stems. She pulled. The prize came away and she drew it, not without some puzzlement at its weight, past the seat slats and on to her knee. She looked across at the women and the old men. Nobody seemed to have noticed.

She glanced down.

'Christ!' murmured Miss Teatime.

On her lap was a clump of polyanthus, vividly yellow and of the proportions of a bridal bouquet. It must have been of recent transplanting and had come up, roots and all, its twenty or thirty blossoms trumpeting her guilt.

Vainly she tried to conceal it behind folded hands. A woman on the right had looked up from knitting and was now staring openly. Miss Teatime dealt her the Christian martyr smile that she had always found immediately effective in afrighting the inquisitive and, left unobserved once more, she looked at her handbag on the seat beside her and tried to decide if it were capacious enough to hold....

'Aha!'

A pair of large black shoes stepped smartly into her field of vision. Trousers. Men's trousers. Oh, God! A park-keeper! She raised her eyes.

'You didn't mean me to miss you, did you?'

The man before her was gazing with ironic admiration at the great plant. He had very pale blue eyes and yellowish eyebrows. Big face, very smooth, almost shiny. Unusually long ears. The hand extended towards the polyanthus was white and backed with a lot of fine, gingery hairs. Its thumb was fleshy but effeminately narrow at the end.

Miss Teatime smiled nervously and slipped her fingers under the plant's roots.

'I suppose you don't happen to have a paper bag or something?'

He took the plant from her and examined it.

'There's a bit of root left on,' he announced. 'You never know, it might take. I tell you what – let's plant it to commemorate our first meeting!'

He swung round towards the earth border and in another moment Miss Teatime was heartily relieved to see the thing glimmering anonymously in the long line of its fellows.

He brushed the knees of his trousers and sat back beside her, half turned against the side of the seat. He put out his hand.

'Jack Trelawney. At your service.'

'How do you do, Mr Trelawney.'

She felt her fingers pressed gently into his palm by the big soft thumb. He did not let go of them, but gave her arm a little wag every now and again during the next five minutes as if to emphasize a point in the conversation.

'And now, Miss Three-Four-Seven....' he paused to gild the little joke with a grin. 'How am I to call you? Three for short?'

'I'm afraid that introductions have never been the happiest moments of my life,' she said wryly. 'You see, my name happens to be Teatime. It really does.'

He looked blank, then hastily summoned an expression of kindly surprise.

'Teatime ... well, well. But how refreshingly different. I like it. I really do.' Her arm was wagged twice. 'And your first name?'

'Lucy. Lucilla, actually, but I think that's a bit Gothic.'

'Oh, Lucy will do very nicely indeed. Lucy Teatime. Yes. I'm so pleased to have met you, Lucy.'

He had a way, she noticed, of lowering his head as he spoke and looking up past those biscuit coloured eyebrows of his. It gave him an air of being serious and confiding. Yet always with a certain sparkle. He was probably used to getting his own way.

'Did you have far to come to meet me?' she asked.

'No, not really. I say, I'm glad it's so fine, though. Perhaps we could have a look at the river later on.'

'That would be lovely.' (Was she ever going to get her hand back?)

'You live in Flaxborough, do you, Lucy?'

'I'm staying here for the time being. It does seem an altogether charming town, from what I have seen of it.'

Her fingers were released.

'Before we go any further, I must make a note of your address.' He was bringing out a folded envelope and a pen with a rolled-gold cap.

Miss Teatime hesitated a second. Oh, well, why not?

'I've put up at the Roebuck Hotel.'

He pouted approvingly. 'Jolly nice berth.' The cap was off the pen. 'What about your own home, though? Your proper home?'

'I suppose I haven't one, really. The house was so huge that it seemed pointless to hang on to it when father passed away. I mean to say – imagine me trying to keep twenty-seven bedrooms aired!'

'All those warming pans!' riposted a chuckling Mr Trelawney.

'Yes, indeed. Anyway, with the sort of ridiculous prices that people are absolutely fighting to pay for Elizabethan manor houses in Berkshire it seemed foolish not to turn it to good account.'

Trelawney swallowed. 'You sold it, then?'

'It's going through,' said Miss Teatime indifferently. She gave a little laugh. 'Who wants nine bathrooms, anyway?'

'I'd rather have nine bean rows and a hive for the honey bee.' A dreamy look had entered Trelawney's pale blue eyes.

'Yeats!' responded Miss Teatime. She sighed happily. 'Do you live in the country, Mr Trelawney?'

'More or less. Actually, I'm rather a bird of passage at the moment. Like you.'

'I see.'

More people had come into the garden. Two of the nearby seats were now occupied. A gangling young clergyman came by, peering at faces. He was wearing bicycle clips and looked, Miss Teatime thought, rather like an ill nourished starling. The boy who had been carted off by his mother appeared to be at liberty once more. Bored, he lounged against the fountain and contrived by putting his thumb over the outlet to send a fine rain over them.

'Belay there, young fellow-me-lad!' cried her companion.

The boy glanced at him contemptuously and sauntered off.

'What they need is a touch of the rope's end,' opined Trelawney. He thoughtfully tugged the lobe of one of his long ears – an action which had the interesting effect of hoisting the eyebrow on the opposite side.

'Have you ... have you any children of your own?' Miss Teatime thought it might be as well to slip in some of the most important questions early. She wished, though, that this one had not sounded like: Do you keep rabbits?

'Not to my knowledge, ma'am, as the Duke of Wellington used to say.'

She laughed politely.

He looked down at his long, plump thigh and flicked away a vestige of soil. 'No, I've never been spliced. I don't think it's fair on a woman, being tied up in port while her husband rolls round the world. Of course, when his sailing days are over ...' he raised his eyes '... that's different, isn't it?'

'So you want to settle down?'

He shrugged and stared past her into the distance.

'A little bit of terra firma, a cottage, slippers by a real, old fashioned fire ... they sound sentimental, I suppose, but you'd be surprised how often they come to mind when you're rounding the Bight or keeping your eyes skinned for bergs away off Iceland or somewhere.'

'Oh, I'm sure they do,' said Miss Teatime comfortably.

He started. 'But you don't want to listen to my little romantic fancies. Tell me something about yourself.'

He reached again for her hand, missed it, and grasped her knee instead. His calm, earnest regard was like that of a doctor impersonally checking cartilage formation.

'I am not sure what I *can* tell you, really,' Miss Teatime said. 'My life has been quite uneventful – rather too sheltered, if anything. You know this is quite a break away for me.

Poor father's accountant ... well, he's mine now, I suppose
... he was most disapproving when I said I was going to leave
everything to him for a while and take a little look round. I
had to placate him by promising I would only draw on my
personal account while I was away.' She gave her melodious
little laugh. 'And I shan't get into much trouble on *that*, believe me!'

Trelawney joined her amusement. Then he withdrew his
hand and looked at his watch.

'Now, then; how about some chow?'

'Chow,' she carefully pronounced, 'would be most accept-
able.'

'I thought we might try a little place I know just the other
side of the station. They do awfully good scampi.'

Deep frozen dogfish tails, Miss Teatime knowledgeably reflected, but she nodded and said: 'Yes, let's.'

Mr Trelawney stood up briskly and with a flourish offered
his arm. They left the garden.

Seven hours later, Miss Teatime sighed and declared: '*Such*
a pleasant day. You really have been very kind, Jack.'

They were in the booking hall of Flaxborough Station and
Trelawney was hooking a return half ticket from his waistcoat
pocket. 'The pleasure has been all mine,' he assured her.

Miss Teatime still did not know where he lived. The point
seemed to have been lost amidst the much more interesting
matters that had cropped up during the afternoon and early
evening. She had gathered, though, that it was somewhere
within fairly easy reach by train and that the train, in fact, was
Mr Trelawney's habitual means of coming into Flaxborough
whenever business (unspecified) or shopping required it.

They had made arrangements for their next meeting and
Trelawney had insisted that she spare herself the chilly tedium
of standing on the platform until the train pulled out. Station
farewells, he had observed, were even worse than embarkations,
which at least had the merit of affording a whiff of good sea air.

So Miss Teatime gave him a smile and a little wave as he
stepped, with naval smartness, past the barrier and disappeared

round the corner of the bookstall; then she turned at once and made her way to East Street.

Entering the Roebuck lobby, she caught sight of the manager's bald head bent over ledgers in the reception office.

'Mr Maddox. . . .'

He looked up, saw her, and ran a great smile of the trade to his masthead (no, really, I must stop this nautical imagery nonsense, Miss Teatime snapped to herself).

'Mr Maddox, a word in private with you, if you would be so kind.'

Fussily he ushered her into the office.

'I am being followed by a police officer.'

'Surely not!'

'There is no doubt of it. Oh, but there is no need to look so concerned. I am quite accustomed to being, as they say, shadowed by the police.'

The manager's frown of anxiety became a gape.

'I thought I'd better mention it,' Miss Teatime went on smoothly. 'These dear people are not invariably as unobtrusive as they – and I – would wish, and if they were to excite a little curiosity it would be only natural.'

'Natural, yes,' echoed the bewildered Mr Maddox.

'I'm so glad you understand. Mind you, my own view is that I am perfectly capable of looking after myself, but you will never persuade police commissioners that in England a woman can be rich and safe at the same time.' She chuckled, as though at a sudden memory. 'Poor old Sir Arthur ... I really think he pictures me as carrying the entire capital assets of Teatime Engineering around in my handbag!'

At this so absurd delusion, Mr Maddox laughed outright. He looked decidedly relieved about something or other.

As soon as Miss Teatime had bidden him goodnight and gone in search of what she termed her 'bedtime unwinder', he took from beneath the blotter the bill he had intended to present to her the following morning. He looked at it, screwed it up and threw it into the wastepaper basket.

Chapter Eleven

PURBRIGHT RECEIVED LOVE'S ACCOUNT OF FAILURE FAR MORE equably than the sergeant had hoped. Not that the inspector was a choleric man – most people, including the chief constable, thought him unnaturally meek for a policeman and one in authority at that. But his mild manner contained a seam of ironic shrewdness against which many a specious or blustering argument had splintered. It was Purbright's 'sarcasm', as those who failed to impose upon him called it, that made stupid people nervous.

'There isn't much you could have done about it, as far as I can see,' he told Love. 'One doesn't expect ladies of gentle breeding to go clambering about back stairs. But we shall have to remember that Miss Teatime has a much sharper eye than we had supposed.'

'She must have a guilty conscience, as well,' said Love, darkly.

'Not necessarily, Sid. None of us cares to be snooped after. Purely on principle, I'm very much against it myself. I think the better of the lady for giving you the slip.'

'Well, that's not....'

The inspector waved aside Love's indignation. 'No, we'll just have to be practical and decide how we can tighten things up.'

'I can't watch both sides of that hotel at once.'

'Hardly.' Purbright turned and examined a town map that was pinned to the wall behind his desk. Having found the Roebuck, he kept a finger on the spot and studied the surrounding lanes. He shook his head.

'No.... I had wondered if there might be a sort of common factor – some place from which she would have to be visible, whichever way she came out. There isn't, though.'

'You could put someone else to watch the back,' Love suggested.

'Laying siege to the place, you mean?'

The sergeant looked blank.

'The trouble is,' said Purbright, 'that there's only Pook to spare.'

In the way the inspector said it, 'only Pook' sounded like a formula in physics expressive of the nearest thing to non-existence.

'You could put him at the back. As a kind of stopper. I mean, if he looked obvious she might think he was the only one and nip back again to the front. So to speak,' Love concluded, doubtfully.

Purbright sighed. 'We can but try. Mind you, there's one bit of encouragement to be drawn. She must have had some good reason to dodge you on this particuar occasion. It does look as if somebody's taken the bait.'

'I only hope he's used to walking.'

There was a knock and the duty sergeant's head appeared round the door.

'A lady's asking if she can see someone about that Miss Reckitt. Will you have a word with her, sir?'

Love departed after holding the door for the entry of a very plump woman in a short yellow coat and thinking that she looked rather like a pot of mustard. Purbright rose and arranged a chair for her.

'You are . . .?'

'My name is Huddlestone. Miss Huddlestone. There was something in the paper about a friend . . . I thought you might tell me what they think has . . . I mean it's something about being missing. Is that right?'

The round, flushed bespectacled face showed strain. Purbright realized that barrel-shaped women had necks too short for looking up in comfort. He went back to his chair and sat down.

'You are a friend of Martha Reckitt, are you, Miss Huddlestone?'

'That's right, yes. I've known her, oh, for years.'

'And you live here in Flaxborough?'

'No, Derby. But I saw about her in the paper.' She was opening a crocodile skin handbag.

'And you're anxious.'

'Well, of course. I didn't know what to think when....' She passed him a cutting without looking up from the bag, in which she continued to search. 'Oh, yes. Here it is.'

Purbright saw she was holding a letter. He glanced at the cutting and handed it back.

'You see, Martha and I don't get together very often nowadays – not like we used to – but we do write to each other every now and then and keep each other up to date with the news. She tells me everything that's been going on. Well, as I say, we're ever such old friends, so that's only natural. But the very last letter she wrote....'

'When was that?'

'Oh, a couple of months ago, I should think.' She looked at all three of the sheets in her hand. 'It isn't dated, actually. January, perhaps.... Anyway, as I was saying, this last letter of hers was quite a big surprise. Knowing Martha, I mean. You see, she'd met this man. Wait a minute ... yes, Giles something-or-other. She doesn't give his other name. And she's actually talking about marrying him....'

'That surprised you?'

'Certainly it did. I mean, I hadn't an inkling that Martha had any ideas in that line. Yet here she is talking about an engagement ring and some cottage this Giles man hopes to take her to. There's just one thing that didn't surprise me – he's a clergyman, apparently. Martha was always dead soft on curates. She was mixed up in a lot of church work, too – Sunday school and that sort of thing....'

'Does she say where this man's church was supposed to be?' asked Purbright.

Miss Huddlestone shook her head. 'I'll let you read this in a minute, but there's nothing in it about that.'

'I ask because inquiries do happen to have been made of

the local church authorities and there is no unmarried clergyman in any of the parishes round about who admits even to
having heard of Miss Reckitt.'

Miss Huddlestone, whose expression had been growing
more animated, suddenly stiffened and looked grave.

'You've been taking this ... this disappearance business
seriously, then?'

'Very seriously, Miss Huddlestone, I assure you.'

She was silent for a few moments. Then she leaned forward
and handed Purbright the letter.

'You'd better see if there's anything there that'll help. I
warn you – some of it's a bit sick-making.... No, no – that's
very wrong of me. It's just that she's never written that sort
of thing before. Oh, Lord! Poor old Martha....'

Miss Reckitt had left her most important news until last:

... and now I must reveal my great secret. If you were here,
of course, you would see it for yourself – or rather the
shining outward evidence of it. Five little diamonds, all in a
row. And on the third finger of this very hand, lying beside
the paper as I write. What do they spell, these five pretty
stones? G-I-L-E-S. Oh, Elsie, he is such an admirable
figure of a man. Strong and gentle at the same time, as befits
a man of the church, and with the merriest of humours
when the occasion suits. The countryside is his greatest love
(next to me, that is, and truly I do not think I flatter myself)
and he has shown me the quite breathtaking little cottage
that he plans to be ours. (From a distance – it is not yet unoccupied.) And guess where it is, Elsie. No, I am not going
to tell you, but I wonder how good your memory is nowadays – suppose I were just to say 'Catch a Crab', where
would you think of? There now – if you are any good at
clues, you will know exactly where Giles and I are going to
live. Talking of the cottage, how glad I am now not to have
touched any of Uncle Dan's money that time when I had a
fancy for a motor car. If we had to wait for the grant that
has been approved by the Church Commissioners, I am sure

someone else would beat us to such a wonderful 'snip', as
Giles calls it (most unclerically, I'm afraid! – but I do understand what he means). Well, Elsie, so much for my great
announcement, and I do hope and pray it pleases you. Now
I must close as I have an important appointment with a
certain gentleman.

Your ever affectionate friend,
Martha.

Purbright raised his eyes to see Miss Huddlestone watching
him anxiously.

'Not much use, is it,' she said.

'Rather less illuminating than I could have wished. There
are one or two interesting points, though.' He glanced once
again over the final page. 'This cottage, now....'

'She doesn't say where it is.'

'She's offered you a clue.'

Miss Huddlestone gave a little puff of derision. 'Oh, that's
typical of Martha. Clues. She loves making mysteries of things.'

'But this one is decidedly odd. "Catch a Crab." Doesn't it
mean anything at all to you?'

She pondered, slowly shaking her head.

'It sounds rather like something to do with rowing,' persisted
Purbright. 'You know – boats. It's when you fall back because
the oar's missed the water. You can't think of an incident of
that kind?'

'I've never rowed a boat in my life.'

That, Purbright reflected, I can believe. He said: 'And
what about Miss Reckitt? Did you ever go on a river with her?'

Again Miss Huddlestone looked dubious. No, she could
remember nothing about rivers or boats.

'Never mind,' said Purbright at last. 'But I should like you
to keep having a go at it in your own mind. Something might
occur to you.'

She promised to persevere.

'Now another thing,' the inspector went on. 'Can you say
anything about this money she mentions?'

'Well, only that it was left her by this Uncle Dan of hers.
I don't think I ever met him.'

'This was some years ago?'

'A fair while. About ten years, I should say.'

'Was it much?'

'Depends what you call much. Three hundred – perhaps
four. But she kept it in the savings bank all the time, so I
suppose there'll be the interest as well now.'

Purbright nodded. There did not seem to be much else he
could learn from Miss Huddlestone. He made a note of her
address and said that she would be informed if and when the
whereabouts of her friend became known. He said nothing of
his own far from sanguine opinion of Miss Reckitt's chances.

Miss Huddlestone trotted stumpily to the door. Purbright
opened it but instead of leaving she stood looking down at one
plump little hand as if wondering however she had got it into
its glove.

'You know, I don't at all like the sound of that clergyman,'
she said quietly.

Purbright pushed the door nearly closed.

'You don't?'

'Partly prejudice, actually. I've never cared for clergymen
very much. Those awful black modesty vest things ... and a
smell of candles and wardrobes. ...'

The inspector waited.

Miss Huddlestone gave a resolute sniff. 'No, they're all right
really, I suppose. But I wouldn't have thought a whirlwind
courtship much in their line. And why should he want to buy
a cottage? I always understood the church provided accommodation.'

'It is usual, I believe.'

'Another thing. I don't want to sound disloyal, or anything,
but let's face it, poor old Martha was no catch. A diamond
ring, for heaven's sake. ...'

'Miss Huddlestone, you said earlier that your friend is keen
on church work and inclined to admire the sort of people with
whom that work would bring her into contact – curates, I

think, you mentioned specifically.'

'Oh, yes. Soppy about them.'

'Do you know of any particular clergyman she was friendly with?'

'Not off hand.'

'Try and think.'

'Well, there is one, but I'm not sure that he counts as a proper clergyman. They do know each other, though. As a matter of fact, he's a young chap from my own home town.'

'Not Mr Leaper?'

'That's him. He hangs out in some tin-pot place in North-gate. I remember him as a kid in Chalmsbury – queer lad with a nose like a carrot.'

So did Purbright. Seven years before, Leonard Leaper had been the junior reporter on the *Chalmsbury Chronicle*, a vocation he relinquished on account of nerve trouble (the editor's mainly, but in part his own) after his discovery of the bomb-shattered corpse of the dreadful Mr Stanley Biggadyke.* The incident had not exactly unhinged Leonard ('He never had a lid in the first place,' averred the editor, Mr Kebble) but it had certainly aggravated an already morbid disposition and sent him, eager for fasts and flagellation, to a crash course in theology offered by an organization called Oxmove – the pro-prietors, if that was the word, of Northgate Mission among others, and publishers of the *Preachers' Digest*.

'The Reverend Leaper,' murmured Purbright ruminatively. He recalled having seen Mr Leaper only the previous day, emerging from the building that held Mrs Staunch's agency.

'I wouldn't place too much reliance on what Len says, mind,' said Miss Huddlestone. 'That is, if you were thinking of. . . .'

'No, I was merely wondering whether there might be some connection. We're still very much at the exploratory stage, I'm afraid.'

'It's this Giles person you want to be looking for,' said Miss Huddlestone firmly. 'And that's for certain.'

* See *Bump in the Night*.

'You may well be right.'

Purbright reopened the door and gave a little bow, then watched her trotting down the corridor.

'You'll not forget,' he called after her, 'about catching crabs, will you?'

Without turning, she raised and wiggled one hand.

Chapter Twelve

DETECTIVE CONSTABLE POOK STOOD FOUR SQUARE IN THE LANE opposite the trade entrance of the Roebuck Hotel and inhaled appreciatively the breakfast smells that drifted from its kitchen. His orders were to make himself obvious and official-looking, and he was carrying them out to the letter.

Shortly before ten o'clock, Constable Pook saw movement in the open doorway of the kitchen. A woman in coat and hat was saying something to two members of the hotel staff. They laughed and made remarks in return. One of them moved aside and the woman came through the door, smiling.

Pook saw that she fitted the description with which he had been provided by Sergeant Love. He braced himself, standing well away from shadows.

Miss Teatime reached the entrance to the small yard and stood still, adjusting her glove.

Pook rocked slightly on the balls of his feet and thrust his hands into the pockets of his raincoat.

Miss Teatime glanced at him indifferently, then turned her attention to the other glove.

Pook rocked some more, hunched his shoulders once or twice, and peered with quite villainous furtiveness up and down the lane. When he looked back at Miss Teatime, she gave him a friendly little smile before looking down to see that all was well with her shoes.

With a flourish, Pook drew a card from his pocket and proceeded to glare at it and at Miss Teatime's face in turns, as if checking a likeness. At the same time, he gave his jaw a twist suggestive of tough resolution and knowledge of a thing or two, and raised one eyebrow so high that the back of his neck began to tingle.

Miss Teatime regarded this performance with every appearance of sympathetic approval for several seconds and then stepped lightly away up the lane.

Pook, appalled, stared at her retreating back.

So far as he could remember, no provision had been made in his briefing for this situation. The woman was supposed to have seen him, guessed immediately his dread profession, and bolted straight back again into the approved area of Love's vigil. But what now?

His first inclination was to plunge through the hotel and seek out the sergeant. But the lane was short and ran into another that offered half a dozen alternative routes of escape. It was essential to keep the woman in sight and that would be past hoping for once he tangled with porters and kitchen maids and the other obstructionists who were sure to be waiting inside the Roebuck. There was nothing he could do. He was stuck with her. Oh, gawd....

Miss Teatime smiled when she heard the heavy tread of her pursuer. But what, she wondered, had happened to the nice pink one? Perhaps it was his day off.

She turned the corner and walked the whole length of Priory Lane before cutting through an alley into East Street, at least three hundred yards farther down from the Roebuck. For twenty minutes or so, she did some leisurely window shopping, gradually making her way towards the big store of Brown and Derehams.

Pook saw her enter the store and he hastened to reduce the distance between them. Inside the doorway he paused to look round the sales floor. The now familiar pink hat caught his attention from about three counters away. He moved closer in.

Miss Teatime led him to the very centre of a large yet somewhat sequestered department before Pook realized that it was given over entirely to corsetry.

He looked about him for some item of merchandise in which his pretended interest might seem even remotely legitimate. There was nothing. Nothing but great cocooned breasts and bellies and bottoms. Had Pook possessed a more poetic con-

sciousness, he might have seen himself as being in the midst
of a monstrous chrysalis collection that the central heating
would eventually hatch into truncated amazons. But no such
intriguing fancy arose to modify his embarrassment.

He was soon looking so guilt ridden that a supervisor went
up to him and asked meaningfully if she could help him. Pook
merely scowled at her.

As the supervisor passed close by Miss Teatime, she raised
her brows.

'They call them fetishists, you know,' Miss Teatime said
sweetly.

After a while, Miss Teatime wandered over to the lift and
stood by the gates. Pook prepared to follow, but strategically
allowed several women to precede him.

The gates opened. Miss Teatime got in, then the women,
and finally Pook. He had to squeeze close beside the operator –
a sallow, resentful girl who accused him with her eyes all the
way to the fourth floor of having designs on her soft furnish-
ings.

At the top, they alighted in reverse order and Pook was
swept for some yards before he could turn and see what Miss
Teatime was doing. She was still in the lift. He pushed back
towards her and was just in time to hear her say something
about having left an umbrella behind when the gates shut and
the lift began to descend. Pook leaped for the stairs.

'Oh, silly me!' exclaimed Miss Teatime two seconds later.
'I didn't bring it today after all.'

The girl viciously threw the lever to 'Stop' and then to
'Up'. 'I wish you'd make up your flippin' mind!'

'I'm really terribly sorry,' said Miss Teatime.

Back on the fourth floor, she left the lift and walked briskly
through the bedroom furniture department, past the cafeteria
and curtainings and down another staircase to the Peel Street
exit.

In the Garden of Remembrance, Miss Teatime found Commander Trelawney (he had reluctantly divulged his rank during

their first meeting, but only when he saw how truly interested she was) slewed round in the seat so that he could look at the flowers in the border.

'It's funny,' he said, 'but already I'm thinking of that one as Our Plant.'

He nodded towards the clump of polyanthus that he had pushed back in the soil. It was distinguishable by the shrunken, droopy appearance of its blooms.

'I think it'll pick up all right.'

'Oh, I do hope so,' said Miss Teatime. 'I'm not late, am I?'

'No, I came a little early today. Business before pleasure. The sooner I can get done with people like bank managers, the brighter the rest of the day looks.'

'They *are* a bit of a bore,' Miss Teatime agreed. 'And so dilatory these days. Don't you think so, or is it just my imagination?'

'I shouldn't call them clippers, certainly. Mind you, one bank can be much nippier than another. And so long as you've got hard cash in the hold, it'll answer the helm quickly enough.'

Miss Teatime smiled and said she supposed he was right. Not that it mattered all that much to her; she never needed to call on big sums and was quite content to leave everything as it was – neatly tied up in 'securities', whatever *they* were.

Trelawney looked amused. 'And do you really not know anything about them?'

'Only that I can't get at them without a fearful amount of bother. A trip to London, for one thing. I have to sign things in person on the spot. And then there's always a teeny glass of Madeira afterwards and everybody is referred to as Mister James or Mister Charles. Oh, you've no idea. . . .'

'But I have, my dear. One of my own companies is just like that. To this day they still hold their annual general meeting in a chop house, with tankards of porter all round and something they call the Chairman's Gammon. . . .'

'Oh, lovely!' cried Miss Teatime.

'. . . and, of course, a quill to sign the minutes . . .'

'Yes, of course!'

'... and would you believe it, nobody can cash a single share without filling in a special requisition that has to be signed by a clerk in holy orders, the headmaster of Eton and the editor of *The Times*!'

'Marvellous!' laughed Miss Teatime. 'Absolutely marvellous!' (Within her merriment was a tiny doubt: the headmaster of Eton ... was that quite the correct title? Never mind, the point was rather trivial.)

They chatted for a while in sustained good humour until Trelawney suggested that a stroll by the river might be a pleasant way of working up an appetite for lunch. Miss Teatime agreed and they entered the series of gently descending streets, lined with old fashioned shops, that led to the Sharms – Flaxborough's harbour district.

This had been once the residential preserve of successful shipping merchants and retired master mariners, but with the ebb of the port's prosperity their big, rather severe looking homes had become tenements or lodging houses. Here and there was one of those depressing English institutions at whose doors and windows can always be glimpsed men in vests and women in curlers and bad tempers, that on the continent would be called brothels.

'Pretty hard tack, this lot,' the commander remarked of a group of inhabitants taking their ease outside a betting shop on the other side of the street. 'That's one reason why I like the country. If you want to leave your doors open, you can, and there's nothing worse than good fresh air can get in.'

Miss Teatime commended his philosophy, but ventured to suggest that there was an even more secure refuge.

'And what's that, Lucy?'

'You ought to know,' she said, giving his arm a gentle squeeze.

'Tell me.'

'A boat. A little ship.' No expectant mother could have referred more coyly to her own embryo.

Trelawney frowned but managed to look indulgent at the same time.

'Oh, but there are lots of practical difficulties, you know. You'd have to have a crew. And, my word, you have to be careful there. Then there are things like ... oh, port dues and so on. And navigation. Have you thought about navigation?'

'Oh, I don't mean a big boat. It was what I believe they call in the trade a forty-footer that I had in mind.'

'I say! You *have* picked up the lingo, haven't you! I should ima....' He stared at her. Their walking slowed to a halt. They had reached the quay and the stern of a rusty old coaster towered above them.

What Miss Teatime readily identified as a roguish smile appeared on her companion's face as he leaned against a bollard and continued to regard her intently.

'Do you know, I believe you've been up to something!' declared the commander.

She smiled up at the coaster's limp red flag. 'I suppose I shall have to tell you. But you mustn't laugh. I won't have you laughing at me, even if I am a poor landlubber.'

Trelawney clapped a hand to one eye. 'Nelson's honour!' he declared, looking more roguish than ever. Then suddenly his face was serious, perhaps even a little anxious. 'Go on.'

'Well,' said Miss Teatime, polishing the clasp of her handbag with one gloved hand, 'it started with father, really. He used to keep a very nice cabin cruiser – a forty-footer, I think he called it – moored on the Thames at home. Of course, during his illness it wasn't used and then when he passed on and there was all that business of the estate being settled I really wasn't in the mood to think about things like pleasure boats.'

The commander nodded sympathetically.

'So I let it go to one of father's old business friends who had often sailed with him and was very keen to have it. I knew what the boat was worth, because it was in the valuation at two thousand three hundred pounds – and that was only just over half what it had cost two years before. But I also knew that Mr Cambridge wasn't terribly well off, so ... well, I made him take it for five hundred. He was quite pathetically pleased

and insisted on giving me an undertaking that if ever he wished
to part with the boat, it would – what is the word – revert? –
it would revert to me for the same money.

'Anyway, I received a letter from Mr Cambridge's daughter.
He is in hospital, poor man, and terribly worried about that
silly promise. And strictly between ourselves, he needs the
money desperately. I wrote at once and told her to sell the boat
for as much as it would fetch, but not for a penny under two
thousand....'

An almost indetectable tremor passed over Trelawney's
face.

'... and now back has come that dear, foolish woman's
reply. No – I must have the boat or no one else will. Final. Flat.
Now can you understand how anyone could be so stubborn?'

The commander's expression said that he certainly could
not.

'Mind you,' Miss Teatime added, 'I must admit that the
temptation is almost irresistible. When I look at that water, I
can just picture the Lucy – did I tell you he named it after
me? – gliding along with that funny little thing on the mast
going round and round....'

'Do you mean to say it's got radar?'

'I don't know what it's called, but it's something to do with
being able to steer in fog. Anyway, she really is a beautiful
little ship and there's nothing I'd love so much as to....'

She stopped, suddenly serious.

'Yes?' Trelawney prompted. Boats had become an altogether fascinating topic.

Miss Teatime remained silent.

'I do believe,' he said, doing his best to be roguish again,
'that you've let out that secret ambition of yours. It's true, isn't
it? You want to cast off.'

She nodded, but something seemed still to be troubling her.

He asked: 'Was it the Lucy you had in mind all the time?'

'Oh, no. When I mentioned my ... my ambition in that
letter, I certainly was thinking of the sea and going to all
those wonderful places like Naples and Marseilles and, and

Mozambique – perhaps with someone to share the adventure. But it was only afterwards, when I got Miss Cambridge's letter, that the idea of the Lucy came into my head. Oh, but no – no, it's impossible. It would be like taking advantage of a sick old gentleman.'

'Come now,' said Trelawney bluffly, 'you mustn't look at it like that. These old chaps are very proud; it wouldn't be kind to go against what they believe to be right.'

'Dear Jack,' she sighed, 'you are so masculine and sensible about these problems. I suppose that comes of your having had to deal with – oh, I don't know – storms and mutinies and all that sort of thing.'

He laughed, and she was smiling, too, but in the next moment she looked glumly into the distance and murmured: 'I don't know why I've told you all this. You see, there is nothing I can do about it, in any case.'

'Simple, my dear. Send Mr Cambridge the money. Ease his conscience.'

'I am afraid you are wrong. It is not simple. I do not have the money.'

Trelawney waved a careless hand. 'How long would it take? A week?'

'Oh, no, longer. Perhaps three. As I told you, my financial advisers are an old fashioned and you might say excessively fastidious firm. They have no faith in any process that takes less than a fortnight. And by then ... well, it would be too late.'

'How do you mean, too late? The man's not dying, surely?'

'Not dying. But in a serious condition in quite another sense. Something called a distress warrant has been applied for by some people to whom he owes money, apparently. Miss Cambridge says that unless the boat is sold within the next week it will be taken from him.'

'Good lord!' Thoughtfully, the commander straightened up from his bollard and took her arm. They strolled in silence towards the lock gates beyond which lay the tidal stretch of the river.

They had almost reached the lock when he stopped and faced her, frowning.

'Suppose,' he said, 'that I were to buy that boat....'

She shook her head quickly. 'He would never let it....'

'Wait, though,' he interrupted. 'Suppose, as I say, that I were to buy it – but in your name....'

'I do not quite understand, dear.'

'In other words, let him think that you are the buyer – at the agreed price, of course – five hundred pounds – when it's really me who's put up the money.'

'But Jack, I could not ask you to do anything of the kind. You do not even know these people.'

'I know you, Lucy, and I think I'm a fair judge of character.'

She looked down modestly.

He took her hand. 'And what would you say if you saw the Lucy bearing down the river here with me at the wheel, eh? Would you be ready to board her for better or for worse?'

'Jack!' Her eyes were shining.

'As a matter of fact, that's just about what I was going to ask you in any case today. About us, I mean. Sailing in convoy.'

It was clear that Miss Teatime was much moved.

The commander gave her hand a reassuring squeeze.

'And now,' he said, 'I'm going to tell you a little secret. Do you know why I happen to have five hundred pounds handy for the doing of good turns to old gentlemen with motor boats?'

He really was so droll. Miss Teatime could not suppress a little giggle.

'I'll tell you why,' said Trelawney. 'Being a very confident cove, I said to myself as soon as I saw you: that dear lady is going to be your lawful wedded, and as such she will want to live in a little cottage in the country! – of course, I didn't know then that you were a sailor! No, a cottage, I said to myself, is what that charming woman will want, and you, Jack, know the very place....'

'Really?' exclaimed Miss Teatime.

'Really. The said cottage is for sale and may be secured, as estate agents say – one did say so this very morning – for a deposit of five hundred pounds. So now you know the little piece of business that brought me into town so early-O!'

'You've paid this deposit already?' She was quite flustered with excitement.

'Not exactly. The cash won't be available until tomorrow. But I came to a firm understanding with the agent. The channel's clear, old girl, absolutely clear.'

'Oh, Jack, how wonderful it sounds!' She paused. 'But the money for the boat ... I mean, how can you use it and still pay that deposit?'

Trelawney took her arm.

'That,' he said, 'is something we shall have to have a little pow-wow about over lunch.'

Chapter Thirteen

AFTER A MEAL WHICH COMMANDER TRELAWNEY DESCRIBED
as 'confoundedly good messing', he and Miss Teatime withdrew to a small deserted lounge where the proprietress of the
Riverside Rest brought them coffee.

Miss Teatime poured, watched by the fond and by now
slightly indolent eye of her companion.

'I love to see you do that,' he said. 'Very womanly. Very
homely.'

'Very ordinary,' corrected Miss Teatime, looking pleased.

'You wouldn't say that if you'd spent your life between
decks and had your tea handed to you in great slopping mugs
by fellows looking like Robinson Crusoe.'

'No, perhaps not.' She passed him a cup.

Nothing of boats or cottages had been said during the meal,
apart from an off hand request by Trelawney to be reminded
of the valuation figure on the Lucy. Two thousand three
hundred, was it? That's right, she had said, with equal indifference.

Now Trelawney scratched one of his long ears, smoothed
back his pale, sand-coloured hair and said that it wouldn't be a
bad idea to get down to a few plans.

'The best thing,' he began, 'would be for me to take the
money down to your friend, Mr Cambridge – or his daughter,
rather – together with a letter from you saying that I'm acting
as your agent. Not cash, mind – it would be silly to carry all
that much on a train journey – but a cheque signed by you....'

'Oh, but the bank....'

He raised a hand. 'I know what you're going to say, but I'll
deal with that in a minute. I'll give Miss Cambridge the
cheque, make sure the boat's seaworthy and bring her up here.
She'll be your property of course....'

'No, Jack. Yours.'

Trelawney made a grimace of good natured reproof.

'You'll never be a business woman at that rate, my love. The deal will be in your name, so the Lucy will belong to you. For the time being, we'll just look on the five hundred as a loan that I'm happy to make.

'Now this point about the bank. You were going to say that you haven't enough to cover the cheque, weren't you? Well, this is what we'll do.

'There's something called a joint account, you see. Lots of husbands and wives have one, and business partners and people like that. We'll go round and open one at my bank, and tomorrow I'll transfer into it the five hundred pounds I was going to use as a deposit on our cottage. Then you can sign the cheque for the boat and it will be drawn on that joint account, all shipshape and Bristol fashion. Do you see?'

Miss Teatime said that indeed she did and thought him terribly good at managing such things. But what about....

'The deposit on the cottage? Ah....' Trelawney beamed at her. 'It so happens that the estate agent is quite an old friend of mine – that's how I got to hear of the place, as a matter of fact – and he'll be perfectly happy to reserve it for me on the strength of my post-dated cheque. That's a cheque which is payable in, say, a month's time. A sort of promise, really, and quite usual.'

'You are sure, Jack? I should not like you to be placed in an awkward situation.'

'Quite sure. And by the time the cheque has to be honoured, your money to repay the five hundred for the Lucy will have come through – you did say three weeks, didn't you? – and been put into our joint account.'

He leaned back, smiling. 'Now then, what do you think of that?'

'Well, it certainly does sound an excellent plan. I had no idea banks could be so accommodating. Mine seems so terribly unapproachable. Perhaps it is because I have never asked about such things.'

'Probably,' Trelawney said.

He looked at his watch.

'I think we'll just have nice time to go round and set things moving.'

Inspector Purbright, blissfully unaware of the failure of the Pook–Love consortium, was looking into the windows of his favourite shops in Northgate as he made his way slowly towards the Oxmove mission hall.

Long before he arrived there, the light breeze carried to his ear the eternal song of the blessed. Did they ever leave the hall for meals, he wondered, or were nutrients administered to them where they stood, as was done for the stalwart and single-minded bellringers of St Luke's, Chalmsbury, into whose mouths were thrust sponges soaked in egg nog and set on sticks.

He entered the gloom of the porch – a sort of corrugated iron Galilee chapel stuck on the main building – and felt for the farther door. Pushing this open, he was met and winded by the full force of the hymn.

The light from three bare electric bulbs hung high in the garage-like roof was reflected stickily from match-boarding walls and from rows of benches that seemed to have been fashioned from treacle toffee. The air was cold and smelled like old women's washstands.

Having regard to the noise, the congregation was incredibly small – a knot of perhaps a dozen at the left front.

Just beyond them, a woman wearing a big black hat jerked backwards and forwards before a harmonium. There was an air of desperation about her; she held down first one lot of keys, then another, then quickly submerged a third bunch – just as though they were a litter of black and white kittens, too numer-ous and too resilient to drown.

The minister, the Reverend Leonard Leaper, stood by the harmonium, leaning lightly upon it and singing like mad.

Purbright advanced a little way down the aisle. He made polite beckoning gestures towards Mr Leaper.

Mr Leaper gave him a cheerful wave and sang even louder.

The inspector again caught his attention and signalled more peremptorily. Leaper abandoned the harmonium and walked up to him. The congregation seemed not to notice the defection; it just went on bellowing on into God's ear.

'Hello there, brother,' greeted Leaper.

Purbright merely nodded. He remembered Leaper's previous existence, as a young newspaper reporter, when it had always been Hello, chief. Obnoxious modes of address seemed endemic to his nature.

They went into the relatively hymn-proof porch.

'I was wondering if you could help me, Len.'

'Fire away, brother.'

'Do you know a woman called Reckitt — Miss Martha Reckitt?'

Leaper's eyes crossed to regard the end of his long, spiky nose; it was his way of aiding thought. 'Yes,' he said after a while, 'I think I do.'

'How well?'

'I used to talk to her sometimes, try to offer her comfort and tidings, brother, tidings.'

'Have you seen her lately?'

'Not of late, I should say. No, definitely not of late.'

'You don't happen to know of any friendships she might have struck up in the last couple of months or so? There's been some mention of a clergyman. First name, Giles.'

Again Leaper's vision converged upon his nose tip, but this time to no avail. 'Of a Giles I know nothing. Or a clergyman, so called? Nix, brother, nix.'

'We understand that Miss Reckitt subscribed to an organization called Handclasp House, a sort of matrimonial bureau. . . .'

'That's right,' confirmed Leaper proudly. 'I advised her to.'

'*You*, Len?'

'I did, brother. And within scripture. Multiply, remember. That's one way of looking at it. The widows of Sidon? Oh, yes, but I'm not to be caught on that. Do you know Sister Staunch?'

'I have met her.'

'A goodly woman. I am glad, brother, to help where I can.'

Good lord, thought Purbright; was this tatter-minded pep-perminty young man a Rasputin to the Staunch's Tsarina? Absurd. Finding him a bit simple, she probably encouraged him to hang around in order to give the impression that her agency enjoyed church patronage.

'And do you know if Miss Reckitt found a friend through this agency?'

'I expect so. She is very deserving.'

'But you don't know for certain?'

'Ah ... No. To that one, no is the answer, brother, and I can't say otherwise. How is Mr Kebble keeping?'

'I really couldn't say.'

'What a pity. I often wonder.'

'Goodbye, Len. Many thanks.'

'Likewise. Go in peace, brother, and cheer-ho.'

At the police station, Purbright found Pook and the sergeant waiting to make confession. He was still feeling the vague light headedness that had been induced by conversation with the Reverend Leaper, and it was a minute or two before he realized what Love, who spoke first, was talking about.

'Oh, Christ, Sid – do you mean to say you've lost her again?'

'It wasn't *me* who lost her,' protested Love.

'But I thought it was your job to follow her?'

'She went out the wrong way again.'

'That's right,' said Pook. 'Straight at me. And I hadn't had any instructions.'

'You were supposed to intimidate her, Mr Pook. Why didn't you? You were the stopper.'

'Well she didn't stop.' Pook's tone suggested a suspicion that the others had known quite well what was going to happen. He had been reading a book lately about double agents.

'And so?' prompted Purbright, more gently.

'I followed her.' There was a short pause. 'Until she lost me in a shop.'

'*She* lost *you?*'

'Oh, yes, it was on purpose, all right. She kept dodging up and down in a lift.'

'Did she, indeed?' Purbright sounded thoughtful. 'Well, we can't do anything about that now. All right, Mr Pook,' he nodded his dismissal, 'don't reproach yourself.' Alone with Love, the inspector stared vacantly at the ceiling.

'This Miss Teatime,' he said at last, 'seems to be quite an interesting character.'

Love gave a short, bitter laugh.

'There would appear,' Purbright went on, 'to be very little to be gained from continuing to play hide and seek with the woman in lifts. She's obviously aware that somebody's following her, and she's astute enough to do something about it.'

'I reckon she's a bit of an old villain,' said Love, irreverently.

'Well, we don't know that. As I said before, I don't blame anybody for dodging narky coppers if they've a mind to. It doesn't mean that they're criminals. But in a case like this, it's not encouraging to have our excellent intentions thwarted by a shrewd and surprisingly nippy female.'

'So what do we do?'

'I've been thinking again about a suggestion of yours, Sid. About taking Miss Teatime into our confidence. I was against the idea before because she seemed likely to be a bit silly and easily flummoxed. On her showing during the last couple of days, she's nothing of the sort. I think she's capable of being very helpful. At the same time, she will have to be warned of the risk she's running.'

'Can I be taken off the long distance lark, then?'

'With pleasure.'

'Thank God for that. By the way, what joy did we get out of that break-in business?'

'Mrs Staunch's office? What I expected. Damn-all. It made Harper happy, though. He's got lots of lovely prints that might have been left by anybody from the window cleaner to the Archbishop of Bombay. It was a bit much to hope for that Rex should turn out to be some felon on file at Central.'

'And the letters to Mrs Bannister?'

'Just smudges.'

'So much for the miracles of forensic science.' Love's feet were beginning to feel better already. A little cynical truculence did not seem too bold a mark of celebration.

Chapter Fourteen

IF THERE WAS ONE THING ABOUT MISS TEATIME THAT seemed predictable, it was her appearance at breakfast shortly after nine o'clock. Purbright decided that this occasion, while perhaps unorthodox, would be the best opportunity of cornering her.

He arrived at the Roebuck at ten to nine and explained his purpose to a very sleepy Mr Maddox, whose stiff morning attire was in curious contrast to the state of its occupant. He appeared to droop within his suit rather like a tortoise inside its up-ended shell.

The manager showed Purbright to a corner table and left him to his own devices after sending one of the waitresses to fetch him a pot of coffee. The inspector tried to decline the coffee, but Maddox said no, it did not do for anyone to sit in the dining room unprovided: the consequent, ah, *lurking* look was not quite, er....

Miss Teatime came through the door at precisely nine o'clock. Purbright felt sure of her identity even before he saw Maddox pass behind her and give a tired nod.

She looked alert and ready to be pleased. Even a glance at the menu, which she took through spectacles that she fished from her handbag and afterwards replaced, did nothing to modify her blandly sanguine expression. A character of some strength, Purbright decided.

He waited until she had finished eating and was pouring out another cup of coffee. Then he crossed to her table and introduced himself.

Miss Teatime showed sign neither of surprise nor of apprehension. She might have been in the habit of breakfasting with inspectors of police every other morning in her life.

'I am pleased to make your acquaintance, Mr Purbright,' she

said, sounding as if she meant it. 'Would you like me to ask the girl to bring you some coffee?' In the way she said 'gairl' Purbright recognized a relic of the well-to-do female education of forty years ago.

'That's very kind of you, but I'd rather not have any more.'

She gave a graceful little inclination of the head and began stirring her own coffee. 'And what is it you wish to talk to me about, inspector?'

'In the first place, I must apologize for the intrusion.'

'Not at all.'

'Oh, but yes. You see, the intrusion has gone more deeply than you are perhaps aware. My appearance this morning is, so to speak, the tip of the iceberg. There have been inquiries – very discreet inquiries, if that is any consolation – into what normally would be rightly regarded as your private affairs. A watchful eye has even been kept on you for part of the time you have been in Flaxborough. Now then, Miss Teatime, don't you think you are entitled to my apologies?'

Her frown was of puzzlement rather than anger.

'It all sounds very intriguing, Mr Purbright, but I am sure you did not come here to work up my indignation against these things you say you have been up to.'

He smiled. 'No, but I thought I'd better prepare you for the explanation which I propose to give now.

'There has been much concern felt here over the disappearance of two local women. They were perfectly respectable and, as far as I am aware, unknown to each other. We don't know if any harm has befallen them, but if not, it seems quite incredible that neither has got into touch with any of her relatives or friends.

'One factor is common to both these cases, Miss Teatime. The women had registered, not long before their disappearance, with a matrimonial agency here in the town called Handclasp House. I'm not going to be obtuse about this – we do know that you have approached the same organization....'

He paused, as if to invite comment.

Miss Teatime, who had been listening intently, one finger

touching her cheek, said simply: 'That is quite true.'

'... and naturally we hope that whatever has transpired will have a happy outcome for you. On the other hand, I think you ought to be on your guard.'

'Against disappearing?' There was a twinkle in Miss Teatime's eye.

Purbright shrugged. 'Both the women who did had recently been successful in finding companionship through this agency. The coincidence cannot be ignored. We think it was the same man in each case and that he was responsible for whatever has happened to them.'

'But you must not stretch coincidence too far, must you, inspector? Are you suggesting that this hard working gentleman has now turned his attention to me?'

'I am suggesting nothing,' said Purbright. 'But I believe that a plausible and dangerous man is using the agency as a means of finding victims. If that sounds a trifle melodramatic, I'm sorry; it just happens to be the only explanation for what has been going on.'

'Then why have you not found him?'

'Because plausible and dangerous men are also as a rule very clever,' said Purbright, a shade defensively.

'Someone must have seen him in the company of these ladies, surely?'

'No one who had reason to be observant. The accounts we have been able to obtain are sketchy, to say the least.'

'You have no indication at all of his identity, then?'

Suddenly her manner relaxed.

'I'm sorry if I seem to be cross-examining you, inspector. You must see, though, that a mere general suspicion could have terribly unjust consequences. Let me be frank. I have met a gentleman through this bureau you are talking about. He impresses me as being kind and honourable. In due course, I shall doubtless learn more about his background. But the relationship is scarcely likely to prosper if I must now regard him as a police suspect.'

The inspector reflected that in Miss Teatime he, like poor

Love, had got rather more than he had bargained for.

'Of course I see your point,' he assured her. 'And if I may say so, you certainly don't impress me as a gullible or incapable person. The fact remains that your – how shall I put it – your qualifications – are exactly those which we could expect to attract the attention of the man we are looking for. For instance, I believe you are not without means. . . .'

'That is so.'

'You are also a newcomer to the district and living on your own.'

'As you can see, Mr Purbright.'

'Yes, well I don't have to spell this out for you, do I? No policeman in similar circumstances would be doing his duty if he failed to warn you.'

She surprised him with a broad, fond smile.

'Of course not, my dear inspector. I appreciate it. But I must beg you not to worry.'

'I shall try not to,' he said drily.

'Good. Now is there anything else I can do for you? Are you sure you will not have coffee?'

'Quite sure, thank you.' He reached to an inside pocket. 'But there is one way in which you can be specifically helpful. This gentleman you say you have met ... oh, what's his name, by the way?'

She hesitated, then shook her head. 'I think, if you do not mind, inspector, that I should keep that to myself for the time being.'

'Are you sure you're being wise?'

'Not unwise, I hope. Ethical, certainly.'

He shrugged. 'As you wish. But at least you can tell me if you have received any letters from him.'

'Naturally. That is how these introductions are effected, you know.'

Purbright placed on the table a slip of stiff white paper on which were five or six lines of writing.

'This is a photographic copy,' he explained, 'of part of a letter which we are satisfied was written by the man who made

contact with the two missing women. Would you mind letting
me see one of the letters you have received from your friend?'

'I should have no objection at all, Mr Purbright, but there is
not one here for you to see. They were simply formal meeting
arrangements. I did not keep them.'

Purbright looked disappointed. 'Mightn't you be able to find
something, Miss Teatime? Even an odd piece or two in a
wastepaper basket would be enough.'

She smiled. 'In an hotel, Mr Purbright, one does not throw
letters into a wastepaper basket. One tears them up and con-
signs them to the toilet.'

'I see. Well, will you take a careful look at this writing and
tell me if you notice any resemblance to what you can remember of your friend's.'

He waited until she had taken out her spectacles, then
handed her the slip.

Miss Teatime scrutinized-it for nearly a minute. She removed her glasses, replaced them in her bag, picked up the slip
and gave it to the inspector.

'Quite, quite different,' she said. 'Of that I am perfectly sure.'

The inspector sighed. 'At least I seem to have been able to
put your mind at rest.'

'Oh, but it was never anything else, Mr Purbright. Not
really.'

When the inspector had gone, Miss Teatime had a nice long
think. Then she left the table and sought out the young lady in
the reception office, whom she asked to recommend a car hire
firm that might be able to oblige her at somewhat short notice.

The girl gave her an address in St Ann's Place. Ten minutes
later, Miss Teatime was on her way there, unfollowed by
policemen.

The garage manager prided himself on an ability to guess,
from his first look at a customer, what kind of a vehicle was
likely to be preferred.

He regarded Miss Teatime judiciously while she made her
request, then nodded like a store Father Christmas and announced: 'Just the very thing for you.'

He led her behind the service bay to an enclosure where about a dozen cars were standing. He went straight to a pale blue Ford Anglia and opened the door.

'Full tank. Key's in. Just drive away. Lovely.'

He shut the door and motioned Miss Teatime to precede him back to the office where minor formalities could now be disposed of.

To his surprise, she stayed where she was.

'Is this the only car which is available?'

'Well ... not exactly, but....'

She stood back, to get a view of the line.

'May I choose from these?'

He shrugged, a prophet without honour.

Miss Teatime scrutinized the row of bonnets in a single, slow-ranging inspection, then stepped forward and placed a gloved finger on the bronze paintwork of a car near the end.

'I shall have this one, if you please.'

The manager gazed dubiously at the low, clean-lined Renault, crouched in the row like some cat-napping athlete.

'I'm not sure you'd find *that* very suitable. It's not English, you know.'

'I am prepared to forego the luxury of patriotism in the interests of comfort and dependability on this one occasion, Mr Hall.'

He made a last effort to redeem his own judgment.

'It's awfully fast,' he said, in the tone wherewith a child is warned to throw away a sweet picked up in the street.

'Good,' said Miss Teatime. 'I should hate to think that all those modifications to the cylinder head and manifold and valve springs and suspension had been wasted.'

The managed closed his eyes and offered a little prayer to the god of garages: *O, please let her hit a lamp-post! Please let these old eyes see her being towed in!*

Even after Miss Teatime had driven off – with depressing obvious proficiency – the man was still so upset that he filed away her agreement form and cheque without noticing that to the latter she had quite forgotten to add a signature.

From St Ann's Place, Miss Teatime drove directly to the
station. She parked the Renault neatly in the forecourt and
went into the booking hall.

On the wall was a table of departures. Miss Teatime donned
her spectacles and took out a pencil and her little memorandum
book.

It was the four minutes past eight train, she recalled, on
which Commander Trelawney had always left for home. She
moved her pencil point down the time-table. Here it was. All
stations to Chalmsbury, then Horley Bank, Stang and Brockle-
stone-on-Sea.

She made a list of all the stops on the route, closed the notebook and put it away.

It was nearly half-past ten.

Buying a platform ticket, she passed through the barrier and
glanced up at the signals beside the footbridge. She was just in
time to see one of the arms lurch to the 'clear' position. A train
from Brocklestone – Trelawney's usual train, she supposed –
was due.

Miss Teatime hurried to the bookstall counter.

'I should like a map of this area, if you happen to have one.
From Flaxborough to the coast is what I want, actually.'

An ordnance survey section? Oh, yes, that would do ad-
mirably. There was no need to wrap it.

The rumble of the approaching train stirred a nearby knot of
people into movement.

Miss Teatime took the map, told an astounded assistant to
keep the change from a pound note, and hurried from the platform just as the train's leading coach went by. Choosing a route
unlikely to be taken by the commander on the way to his bank,
she was out of sight of the station entrance before the first passenger off the Brocklestone train emerged.

Today's meeting was to be half an hour later than the usual
eleven o'clock. Miss Teatime debated whether she should risk
taking a quick whisky or two first ... (I felt so foolish, Jack,
having to sit down on the stairs while this man brought me a
glass of something to pull me round – I do believe it was

spirits). . . . No, better not, perhaps.

When she reached the Garden of Remembrance, she walked past the gate and turned instead up the path flanked with yew and cypresses that led to the porch of St Laurence's. She entered the church and sat down near the back. In the cool, grey solitude, she unfolded the map and supported it on the back of the chair in front of her.

She studied it for nearly half an hour.

Chapter Fifteen

THE CLOCK IN THE TOWER OF ST LAURENCE'S CHURCH STRUCK
falteringly. It was half past eleven. Miss Teatime looked away
from the drinking fountain, at which she had been watching
a little girl methodically scrub out her doll's clothes, and
gazed towards the garden entrance. There was no sign of
Trelawney.

She felt a twinge of anxiety. Up to now, he had shown himself an almost aggressively punctual person. Behaviour out of
character was one of the very few things that made Miss Teatime nervous. It tended to upset calculations, and earning a
living was difficult enough these days without one's having to
re-cast the horoscope, as it were.

However, two minutes later she saw the commander's fair
hair bobbing along beyond the hedge. He pushed open the gate
and strode towards her. Even while he was still twenty yards
away, she could see from the set of his head and the briskness
of his step that he was in a good humour.

'A thousand apologies, dear lady. I was prepared to find you
flown.'

'Nonsense, I have only just arrived myself.'

'Excellent!' He patted her thigh, as he might a gun dog. 'In
any case, I've a perfectly good excuse in my locker – or rather in
ours, as it's a joint account. The money's paid in – five hundred
nice shiny Jimmy O'Goblins!'

(Dear God! Where had she last come across that one?
Sapper? Henty?) She widened her eyes commendingly. 'My
word! You are not one for wasting time, Mr Trelawney.'

'Hello-o-o. . . .' Mock despair was on his face. 'Who's this
talking to *Mister* Trelawney?'

'Commander,' she corrected mischievously.

'What! Pulling rank now, eh?'

Her glance fell. 'Jack. . . .'

'I should jolly well think so!' Again he patted her thigh, but this time his hand remained. He gazed closely into her face while his fingers contracted. She was about to draw sharply away when she saw in his eyes genuine interest and surprise.

'I say. . . .' He withdrew his hand and stared at where it had been. '*You've* got some muscle, haven't you?'

Miss Teatime straightened her skirt. 'I do try and keep in trim, as a matter of fact. Just a few toning up exercises.'

His air of bright purpose returned. 'Did you write that letter?'

Opening her bag and holding it so that the map she had bought that morning stayed out of sight, she took out an envelope and handed it to him.

'The cheque is there as well,' she said. 'I have made it out to the daughter just in case there is some difficulty in Mr Cambridge's dealing with it in hospital.'

He nodded. 'Very sensible.'

The envelope was unsealed. He drew out the letter and began to read.

Dear Evelyn [Miss Teatime had written],

This is to introduce my good friend, Commander John Trelawney, who has kindly agreed to act on my behalf in the matter of the boat. He will hand you my cheque, which, as you will see, is for five hundred pounds (I wish you would let me make it a sum nearer the true value of the Lucy, or even half of it, but it seems that you and your father have made up your minds). Please give Commander Trelawney the receipt, and also the boat's manual and the other documents – of which you will know more than I – and take him to the mooring. He is going to sail the Lucy here himself (a task for which I could scarcely have chosen anyone better qualified than a one-time Naval officer!) and he will wish, of course, to satisfy himself that she is in good condition for the voyage. I think there is nothing much to add, except perhaps the telephone number of my hotel (Flaxborough

2130), in case you wish to ring me about any details I have
forgotten to mention. I do hope and pray that the money,
ridiculously inadequate as of course it is, will be of some
immediate use in easing your troubles.

Yours sincerely,
Lucilla.

Trelawney looked up. 'I should say she is very lucky to have
such a good friend,' he said solemnly.

'Just as *I* am,' replied Miss Teatime, with no less sincerity.
He put an arm round her shoulder and squeezed in a
comradely fashion.

'Now how do I find this good lady?'

'Do you know Twickenham?'

'Only as a rugger ground, I'm afraid. I used to go down for
the navy matches whenever I happened to be ashore.'

'I do not think that would be very near where the Cambridges live. Their address is on the envelope, by the way.
It is a rather nice old house in a place called The Turnills.
Number eight. It is not so much a street as a sort of close,
with the river at the lower end. Ask anyone for the old part
of Twickenham and you should have no difficulty in finding
it.'

'Is there a station handy?'

'Your best plan probably will be to go to Richmond Station
and cross the river. It is a pleasant walk and not very far.'

'Fine.' He put the letter in his pocket.

'When do you intend to go?'

'Tomorrow morning. There's a London train just before
ten o'clock.'

'I shall see you off,' announced Miss Teatime, with an air
of sudden decision.

'Oh, you don't need to trail round specially for me.'

'But I shall, Jack. I know you are going up by train, but I
cannot help thinking of you as embarking on a voyage. After
all, it will be a voyage back – a real one. Are you not afraid of
storms?'

Trelawney could not help laughing. For a moment, Miss Teatime looked abashed, then she joined in his amusement.

'You must think of me waiting here like Madame Butterfly,' she said. 'I wonder if there is a hill top from which I can watch out for you.'

'O-o-one fine da-a-ay!' sang the commander, not to be outdone in drollery.

Miss Teatime sighed. 'It all seems like a dream,' she murmured.

'Yes, doesn't it. . . .'

'It sleeps four, you know. *She* does, rather.'

'She?'

'The Lucy. And there is the loveliest little kitchen.'

'Galley, my dear.'

'Of course. Galley. You will not believe this, but I am really a very good sailor.'

'I do believe you.'

'Do you think we shall be able to sail in her all the year round?'

He smiled. 'Hardly. At least we shall have to winter in our cottage.'

'Yes, the cottage. . . . Tell me about the cottage, Jack.'

'You shall see it for yourself very soon. White walls – thatch – little windows under the eaves. *And* central heating!'

'Marvellous!'

'And scarcely a soul within hail.'

'Whereabouts is it, Jack?'

'You'll see.'

'Tell me.'

'That's enough, my girl. You're sailing under sealed orders. Just leave everything to the navigator!'

'What an old tease you are!'

That evening, after she had waved goodbye to Trelawney when he looked back from the other side of the ticket barrier, Miss Teatime did not immediately leave the booking hall.

She waited, listening for the arrival of the Brocklestone train. Only when she had heard the last of its departing coaches rattle over the level crossing at the station's east end, did she walk out into the forecourt and make her way to the car.

She got in and put the map on the seat beside her, together with the list of the train's stopping places.

The first of these was Pennick, a village just beyond the outskirts of Flaxborough, whose expansion would eventually absorb it as a suburb.

The Pennick road ran almost parallel to the railway. Its first mile, while fairly free of traffic at this time of the evening, was lined with houses and shops. It was within the speed restriction area, and Miss Teatime was careful to observe the limit, give or take twenty miles an hour, until she saw the crossed white discs at the beginning of a comparatively sparsely built-up stretch of ascending road. Then she let the Renault hum happily into the eighties.

A series of three sharp double bends constrained her to drop gear and halve the car's pace, but on emerging from the last corner she found herself at the start of a straight descent into Pennick village.

The station could be seen quite clearly. It stood on its own, a little to the right of the village and connected to its main street by a fenced path. The train from Flaxborough was just drawing in.

Ten seconds later, Miss Teatime's car stopped precisely opposite the station path.

The first passenger was coming out of the door of the little booking office. A woman, carrying a shopping basket. Two young men followed, then another woman with a little girl. No one else. Behind a window in the station, a shutter-like movement of light and shade grew faster and faster; then suddenly the window showed clear daylight. The train had gone.

Hambourne was its next stop, about two miles farther on. The map suggested the road to be fairly free of complications. Miss Teatime set off again.

Once beyond the last of Pennick's cottages, she saw with surprise just how straight the road was. It might have been built as a third rail track. Hambourne was actually in view, a tiny cluster of russet-coloured roofs, glowing in the last of the sun.

Here it would have been simple enough to pass the train, but she decided against doing so. Rail passengers had nothing to do except look out of their windows and even at twenty or thirty yards it was not difficult to recognize the driver of an overtaking car. So she drove slowly into Hambourne and again was able to pick a vantage point near its station before any travellers made an appearance.

There were two. Neither was the commander.

She drew another blank at North Gosby.

Between there and Strawbridge, she encountered an almost disastrous hold-up in the form of a flock of sheep that was being driven along the road to fresh pasturage. This lost her five minutes, and only a hazardous, if exhilarating, passage through Gosby Vale at a fraction over ninety saved her from missing Strawbridge's homecomers altogether.

By the time she reached Moldham it was decidedly dusk and she was alarmed to find that the railway line, together with Moldham Halt, had somehow contrived to put between themselves and the road a broad and seemingly bridgeless canal. Helplessly, she watched the train come to a stop on the far side of the water.

Then, almost at once, it moved on. She had not heard a single door slam. Moldham, apparently, had sent none of its sons and daughters to the big town that day.

Miss Teatime switched on the lamp behind the driving mirror and consulted her map.

Only Benstone Ferry now, then Chalmsbury Town. It true that the train went on from Chalmsbury to Brocklestone, but that was nearly thirty miles farther on. Surely Trelawney did not come all *that* way to press his suit? No, at Chalmsbury she would call it a day.

Darkness steadily deepened as she drove the five miles to

Benstone. It spread out from the hollows in the fields and gathered beneath hedges. The road, winding now, and with a disconcerting way of slipping suddenly away to right or left as if alarmed by her headlights, was of the greyness of grey cats. She could defeat it only by remaining constantly alert and using the lower gears to whip the car into pursuit of every advantage that its lights revealed. The Renault's cornering, she told herself happily, was tight as a turd in a trumpet.

Even so, on such a road at this time of day there was no better than an even chance of reaching Benstone Ferry before the train. Would there still be a waterway between her and the line? She would need to have another look at the map as soon as she got to the village.

A long mass of darkness loomed up on her left. She was passing a plantation. A brown blob moved erratically from the side of the road ahead. It was in her path, creeping first one way and then another. She braked, dropped into second gear and skirted round it, smiling at the glimpse she had had of tiny eyes and a wet boot-button snout. Hedgehogs, she considered, were very endearing creatures.

Against the glimmering west, the black peaks of roadside cottages began to appear. An isolated street lamp's yellow rays fell upon the signboard of an inn ... George the Fourth, tight-collared and archly surprised, a great pale blue, bejewelled, silk-bound dropsy in the sky. Farther on were the lighted windows of four shops and a cabin in which a group of Benstone villagers stood waiting before a fish and chip range.

Miss Teatime pulled up and held the map in the light from the cabin. The station was about a quarter of a mile away, along the next road on the right. And this side, thank God, of the canal – here called the Benstone Eau apparently.

She made the turn and almost at once saw the train's lights, a distant golden chain moving slowly to the left. From the station, just visible at the far end of her headlamps' beam, four or five people were walking up the lane towards her.

They drew to the side to let her pass and she scanned their faces. Strangers.

Then she spotted a figure on its own, moving past the corner of the station. She recognized Trelawney as he stooped to unlock the door of a car.

Miss Teatime drove straight past, continued for about a hundred yards, and stopped just beyond a gateway, into which she reversed. As soon as she saw Trelawney's car emerge from the station yard and turn towards the village, she swung back on to the lane and followed it.

In Benstone, the other car crossed the main road and gained speed down a hill. Miss Teatime kept a fifty-yard distance from the two red tail lights. These flickered every now and then, presumably when the car went over one of the frequent patches of uneven surface.

The descent ended in a left turn, after which the road climbed steeply for a while before levelling off between what seemed to be stretches of common. Another turn led them past a grove of silver birch and down into the valley of a stream.

It was at the moment when the commander's car reared to cross a hump-backed bridge over this stream that its tail lights winked twice and died. Miss Teatime accelerated to close the gap but by the time she reached the bridge the short stretch of road between it and the next corner was empty.

The rest of the climb from the valley was so tortuous that only an occasional white glow among the trees indicated that Trelawney, who obviously knew the road well, was still ahead.

At the top, Miss Teatime found herself in high, open country. Not far away, skeins of cold violet light evidenced the main streets of a town. Chalmsbury, no doubt. But where had dear Jack got to?

There.... She saw the narrow, rather weak beams lift and fall, swing round, turn again....

Odd. They had gone out.

She drove on to where she thought Trelawney's headlights had last been visible, but realized how difficult the darkness made her judgment. On her left was the opening to a little lane. Farther on was another turning. And on the opposite side of the road, a third. He could have gone up any of these.

Pulling up, she quickly switched off the engine and opened the window. She listened intently. A faint throbbing came to her for a few seconds only, but from what direction she could not be sure. Then, distantly, the sound of a closing door. Silence.

She put on the mirror light and traced on the map the journey she had made from Benstone Ferry. The common, the valley with the stream, the bridge ... the route was quite easy to follow. And so – her finger moved on – she must now be exactly ... yes, here. She pencilled a ring round the three little side roads.

Miss Teatime leaned back in her seat and considered. She was certainly not going to traipse around on foot in the darkness. At least she knew now where to come. Ten minutes in daylight would be enough for finding out the rest. If that proved necessary. It might not, of course. She knew better than to be greedy. Particularly in this case. Goodness, yes. If all went as it should tomorrow, she would leave well alone. If not ... well, a girl had to live and there was more than one way of skinning a cat.

Chapter Sixteen

COMMANDER TRELAWNEY LEANED FROM THE CARRIAGE WINDOW and blew a kiss to the receding figure of Lucy Teatime. Not until she was out of sight, lost in the straggle of hesitant, slightly embarrassed seers-off on the Flaxborough up platform, did he withdraw his head, close up the window and sit down.

The train was that recommended by Flaxborough booking clerks as 'the best of the day' – a testimonial that might have had a brighter ring had it not sounded, in their mouths, synonymous with 'the best of a bad lot'. In fact, it was quite reliably fast and comfortable and a good deal cleaner than expresses from more notable centres of population.

The commander had lunch 'aboard', as he would have said if Miss Teatime had been there, and filled in the rest of the time before the train's arrival at Euston by reading a boat-builders' catalogue which had arrived for him by that morning's post.

He was surprised and more than a little gratified to learn how expensive a relatively humble river craft was. The more ambitious models were comparable in price with the best makes of motor car. As for the builder's largest and most lavishly equipped offerings, these were illustrated without mention of such vulgar irrelevancies as cost, but it was obvious from the scale up to that point that the four thousand mark was by no means high water.

It was nearly two o'clock when Trelawney left the train and took a taxi to Waterloo. London was colder than he had expected. The sky was full of low, curd-like cloud, driven by a wind that swooped fitfully into the streets and set grit and bus tickets swirling in the shop doorways.

By the time he came out of Richmond Station, a fine rain was being blown in from the direction of the river. He kept

in the shelter of shops as much as possible until he reached
the bridge. At the sight of its gleaming parapet and the sound
of bus tyres hissing at the heels of what few pedestrians were
braving the crossing, the commander reeled back beneath a
café awning and prepared to hail the next taxi to come in
view.

His third sortie was successful. As he hunched thankfully
in the dry, leather-smelling gloom, he caught a glimpse of the
river over which the cab was carrying him, and groaned. It
made him think, for a moment mercifully brief, of what the
sea was in all probability like.

And now here he was, he supposed, in Twickenham. He
watched the passing scene. It might have been Acton, or
Streatham, or Balham, or Reading. Or anywhere. What did
names mean here? Why did people still pretend that there
were individual oats in this great bowl of porridge?

But when he got out of the taxi and saw the deserted, gently
curved street of Georgian houses, each with a little railed
garden into which raindrops splashed from the boughs of old,
imperturbable sycamores, he had to admit that homogeneity
was not yet absolute even in Middlesex.

He found number eight The Turnills half way down the
right-handed terrace – the taxi had been unable to enter the
street because of three bulbous iron posts set across the car-
riageway at its upper end.

His knock was answered by a slim, fair-haired girl of eleven
or so, whose glasses gave her small, fastidious-looking face an
attractive air of solitude.

'How do you do?' she inquired of him, seemingly anxious
to gain a truthful reply.

'Good afternoon,' said the commander, with a big is-your-
mother-in smile. 'Do some people called Cambridge live in
this house?'

'Yes, they do,' said the girl. (A neighbour's child, perhaps?
A runner of errands?)

He peered down amiably. 'I should rather like to speak to
them. To *Miss* Cambridge, that is.'

'I am Miss Cambridge.'

The commander laughed. 'No, no. Miss Evelyn Cambridge, I mean.'

'But that's me. I'm Evelyn. What is *your* name, please?'

'Well, fancy that.... No, I'm afraid I haven't made myself very clear. My name is Commander Trelawney and I wish to speak to the *other* Miss Cambridge – the lady who is the daughter of old Mr Cambridge.'

The girl considered this, her natural politeness prompting her to attempt some interpretation that would satisfy the visitor. The best she could muster was: 'I don't think Grandad had a daughter called Evelyn, but I'll ask Daddy if you like.'

'Daddy?'

'Yes. He's called Mr Cambridge, as well.'

'Ah ... well, perhaps if I were to have a word with him....'

The girl turned, then looked back at Trelawney apologetically and pulled the door fully open. 'I should have asked you to come in, shouldn't I?'

'That is most kind of you, my dear.' He stepped forward and stood within the doorway.

After giving him a careful glance, as if to make sure that he fitted properly and would not fall over when left alone, she trotted off down the corridor and disappeared round a corner at the end.

The commander stuck his hands in his pockets and stood frowning out at the rain. He told himself that the apparent surplus of Cambridges was nothing to worry about. The child, no relation at all but simply avid for security and affection, was doubtless identifying herself with Lucy Teatime's friend. 'Daddy' would prove to be another dream figure – an imaginary father whom she pretended to consult when difficulties cropped up. Poor child. At any moment now, the real Miss Cambridge would come out and....

He turned, having heard a gentle scuffling noise. Also he was vaguely aware of being watched.

He peered along the corridor. As his eyes grew accustomed

to the dimness, he discerned a number of small figures. They were ranged, apparently in some order of seniority, in a shadowy doorway and were gazing at him with dark, serious eyes. They reminded him for an instant of an unpacked nest of Japanese dolls, the sort that fit one inside another. But before he could begin to count them, they flitted away out of sight.

The commander's frown deepened. There was something very odd about all this. Why had Lucy not mentioned that the house would be full of children? Were they old Mr Cambridge's? A hobby, perhaps, that had finally landed him in his present financial predicament. Into hospital, too. Yet surely the brood didn't belong to his daughter? The straight-laced Lucy was hardly likely to have fostered the friendship of an unmarried mother – least of all one whose irregular habits were of such patent regularity....

His anxious musing was brought to an end by the appearance of a man of pleasant aspect and with much the same expression of bespectacled helpfulness as the girl.

The man greeted him affably. His voice resembled that of a don, delighted to discover at his door a colleague bearing port.

'My name is Cambridge,' said the man.

To Trelawney, the announcement sounded like some elaborate pun. He felt by now thoroughly bewildered.

'Come along in,' said Mr Cambridge, leading him through a door on the right into a large, warm room that seemed at first sight to be a musical instrument museum. He waved him to a chair.

'My daughter says that you are Commander Trelawney.'

The commander nodded. He said, a little falteringly: 'I'm very glad to see you're ... out of hospital again.'

'Hospital?'

'Haven't you been in hospital?'

'Not for some years, no.'

'Oh.... I'm sorry – I must have misunderstood. Anyway, you're looking very fit. I'm glad.'

Mr Cambridge gave a little bow. His face remained calm. Wasn't he bearing bankruptcy rather too well?

'I have come about the boat,' announced the commander.

There was a short silence.

'But I don't think we want a boat,' Mr Cambridge said. He looked at the door and added: 'I'll ask my wife, if you like.'

Trelawney tried not to believe that a horde of impostors had taken advantage of the removal of the real Mr Cambridge to hospital and seized his house.

'I am not selling boats,' he said. 'I am here to buy yours.' He reached in his pocket for the letter. 'On behalf of its original owner.'

'A boat,' Mr Cambridge repeated thoughtfully. He looked up. 'You're sure you don't mean a cello?'

Trelawney stared wildly.

Mr Cambridge stepped to a corner of the room where there was, indeed, a great fat stringed instrument. He stroked it fondly. 'Edwin can't really manage it, you know, and Estella's got her hands full with a harp at the moment. I don't like to see it go, but. . . .'

Trelawney cut him short by leaping up and thrusting the letter into his hand.

Mr Cambridge looked at it. 'But this is addressed to Evelyn. She's the one who let you in, you know.'

'Read it.'

Mr Cambridge slit open the envelope.

'How very odd,' he said, three minutes later.

Trelawney took back the letter and put it in his pocket. He continued to regard Mr Cambridge in grim silence.

'There obviously has been some misunderstanding, Mr Trelawney. To me, that letter is quite incomprehensible. I'm awfully sorry.'

'Then you don't know this ... this woman?'

'I have never even heard of her.'

Trelawney nodded. He looked very angry indeed.

When he had gone, Mr Cambridge sorted among the children until he found Evelyn, whom he led by the hand into the room with all the musical instruments.

'Tell me, Evelyn,' he said, 'do you know a lady called Miss Lucilla Teatime?'

'Yes,' said Evelyn.

'And who is she?'

'I don't know *who* she is, but I can tell you where she used to live.'

'All right.'

'Three doors up, on the other side. She was very nice.'

'But is she there now?'

'Not now. She went away. She said she was going to get married to Mr Jackman. He keeps that jeweller's next to the paper shop at the top.'

'I see.'

'But I don't think she ever did.'

Once the commander had been borne away on Flaxborough's best train of the day to London, Miss Teatime quitted the platform and went at once to the Field Street branch of the Provinces and Maritime Bank.

As she entered, she received a nod of recognition from the clerk with whom she and Trelawney had arranged the opening of their joint account two days before. She smiled back at him and drew a chair to a small table set against the wall.

The clean, sharp-edged cheque book positively creaked with newness when she folded back its cover. Only one cheque had been used; it was now on its way to Twickenham. Little girls were lucky these days, Miss Teatime told herself. No one had travelled across half England with an order for her to be paid five hundred pounds when she was a child. The only bouncy thing *she* had ever been brought was a ball.

She dated the next cheque in the book and wrote 'cash' in small, maidenly copperplate. Amount ... now what should she put? To lift the full sum of dear Jack's transfer of the previous day was feasible but crude. There were no grounds, of course, on which it could be challenged. The account was hers no less than his. And yet.... No, taking the whole lump would be as bad as wiping up gravy with a piece of bread. There was too much wolfish behaviour in the world today.

She appended her neat signature, filled in the counterfoil and carefully tugged free the cheque.

'Good morning, Miss Teatime.'

(Her name remembered on only the second occasion? What a conscientious young man. What a nice bank.)

'Good morning, Mr Allen.' The name was engraved on a bronze plate set above the grille. (Bronze, not plastic: the employees of *this* bank were clearly no fly-by-night journeymen.)

Mr Allen picked up the cheque, glanced at it in the most cheerfully matter-of-fact way, and nodded. 'Four ninety-seven, eighteen and six. Yes ... I shan't keep you a moment, Miss Teatime.'

He wheeled off his stool and disappeared through a door in the partition behind him.

Two minutes later, he was back, brisk and obliging as ever. But he was no longer holding the cheque.

He leaned forward, smiling. 'If you will just go down to that end of the counter, Miss Teatime' – his head gave a slight tilt to his left – 'Mr Beach will look after you.'

She looked in the direction indicated and saw a plump, friendly-seeming man standing twenty feet away. He beckoned her benignly, and showed her into an office. The office, with its orange carpet, glass and aluminium table, and long, bottle green velvet curtains, looked more like an advertising agent's gin parlour.

Miss Teatime accepted the proffered chair. Mr Beach took his seat behind a desk of maple, inlaid with what appeared to be white porcelain lozenges, each initialled 'P & M'.

He made of his fingers a prayer-pyramid and looked under it at Miss Teatime's cheque, lying on a blotting pad.

'Now, Miss Teatime, I take it that you wish to withdraw a sum of four hundred and ninety seven pounds from the account which you have jointly with Mr Trelawney.'

'I do, yes.'

'You are aware, I expect, that a customer with a bank account – any kind of account – may not take out more money than there is credited to that account?'

There was a pause.

'Mr Beach, I really do not see any need for irony. It is pure coincidence that matters in connection with our business – Mr Trelawney's and mine – have arisen which necessitate this withdrawal so soon after the money was deposited. But, after all, it is *our* money, Mr Beach, and. . . .'

She stopped. Of course she knew what had happened. It was only some kind of professional reflex action that had made her pretend ignorance and indignation.

Mr Beach raised his eyes.

'How much did you suppose this account contained?' he asked.

Miss Teatime appeared to think for a moment.

'Five hundred and five pounds. Oh – less ten shillings for the cheque books, I suppose.'

'I regret to say that you are under some misapprehension, Miss Teatime. Deducting the cheque book charges – ten shillings, as you say – there remains of the original deposit exactly four pounds ten shillings.'

She stared.

'But ... but Mr Trelawney called yesterday in order to transfer five hundred pounds from his personal account into this one.'

'If that was his intention, I'm afraid something must have prevented his coming in,' said Mr Beach. He sounded very sympathetic.

'Dear me. . . .'

'Oh, you mustn't worry about it, Miss Teatime. We are quite used to these small misunderstandings. They happen, you know, they happen. Even in the best regulated circles, I assure you. . . .' (Oh, for crying out loud, thought Miss Teatime.) 'The bank is not embarrassed. We are aware of how busy people are nowadays and how easily things slip their memories. In all probability – in all probability, I say – Mr

Trelawney will be calling in some time today and then we can....'

She rose, ignoring the cheque that Mr Beach had begun to wave diffidently in her direction.

'All I can say about Mr Trelawney,' she interrupted firmly, before walking to the door, 'is that he has a pretty piss-boiling way of going about things.'

Chapter Seventeen

IT WAS THE FOLLOWING MORNING THAT A LETTER WITH A Derby postmark and addressed to Inspector Purbright arrived at Flaxborough police station. He opened it eagerly.

About that little talk we had, [Miss Huddlestone had written], and the thing you asked me to try and remember — well I have puzzled it over and all of a sudden today it came to me what Martha (Miss Reckitt) meant by Catching a Crab.

When we were children and both living in Chalmsbury we went for walks a lot and often brought back fruit and things for our mothers to make jam. Well there was a cottage not far from my home, out towards Benstone Ferry, and it had a big garden with fruit trees. An old lady lived in it then and we noticed that she didn't pick the fruit much, so one day we knocked and asked if we could take some apples. She said Oh they are just crabs, you know, so we said we wouldn't bother. Actually we thought she wasn't quite right in the head and when we got home I told my mother that a funny old woman had made out that she had crabs in the garden, just as if it was the seaside. And mother said don't be so silly, she just meant crab-apples and they were very good for jelly. Anyway we went back and got some, and the next year as well, but we often had a good laugh over getting that idea about crabs. Of course Martha would remember it straight away when this man took her to see it. It was called Brookside Cottage and the last time I saw it it had been done up a good deal and had a garage and that sort of thing. It stands on its own at the end of a lane — Mill Lane I think we used to call it —about two miles out of Chalmsbury on the Benstone Road. I do hope this is some use to you and that you soon find what has happened to poor Martha.

Purbright opened a drawer in his desk and took out a copy of the same ordnance survey section as Miss Teatime had bought on the station bookstall. The ring he pencilled on his, though, was smaller and more precise than Miss Teatime's reference.

He went to the door and called in Sergeant Love.

'This' – he pointed to the ringed cottage – 'is the place that Martha Reckitt's intended said he was going to buy for her. He probably told the same story to Mrs Bannister. The address is Mill Lane, Low Benstone, and the cottage used to be called Brookside, although there's no guarantee that it still is.

'There are two possibilities. Either the chap just picked the place at random as part of his scheme to string those women along, in which case he's probably never even made an inquiry about it. Or it is genuinely for sale and he had some reason for knowing it. There's just a chance of some connection. We'll have to work on it.'

'You mean I will,' Love observed, without malice.

'For a start, yes. I've got this Teatime woman coming in this morning. You'd better try the estate agents first. Find out if the place is for sale, which agent is handling it, who the owners are and whether they are still living there.'

'Just the Chalmsbury agents?'

'They're the most likely, but if you draw a blank there you'll have to ask around in Flax as well.'

The sergeant left to provide himself with a classified telephone directory and a mug of tea.

Just before ten o'clock, Miss Teatime was shown in to Purbright's office. The inspector fancied that her manner had a slightly more purposeful edge to it than when he had last seen her. And, indeed, she came straight to the point.

'I have given some further thought, Mr Purbright, to the matter we discussed the other morning, and I have decided that I might have been just the tiniest bit over confident in one respect. That is why I telephoned and asked to see you again.'

'I'm very glad you did, Miss Teatime. What has been worrying you?'

'Oh, not worrying, exactly, inspector. I am quite sure in my own mind that what I said then was true. But I cannot help feeling that the assurance I gave you about that handwriting was accepted by you more out of politeness than conviction.'

'I took your word for it, naturally.'

'Ah, yes; but I know that my word is not really evidence.'

'Not scientific evidence, perhaps.'

'No. And so for the sake of everyone concerned – my friend by no means least – I intended to try and give you an actual example of his writing.'

'I see.'

'It will be best, do you not think so?'

'I'm sure it will.'

Miss Teatime nodded and picked up her handbag and gloves. She regarded the inspector for a moment in silence, then smiled.

'Do you know, I really think you are anxious about me, Mr Purbright.'

'I am,' he said simply.

'There is no need to be.'

Purbright leaned forward. 'Look, won't you tell me now the name of this man?' His face was serious.

She appeared to consider. Then she said: 'I am sorry, but I must ask you to wait a little longer. Where can I reach you at eight o'clock this evening?'

He looked surprised. 'At home, I hope. Why?'

'What is the address?'

'Fifteen Tetford Drive.'

Screwing up her eyes, she wrote it in her little notebook.

'And now may I have that photograph? The handwriting, you know.'

He took it from the folder at his elbow and handed it across the desk. She put it into her bag.

Purbright watched her get up and wait for him to see her to the door. Then he, too, rose.

'I hope you know what you are doing,' he said quietly.

She gave him a bright smile of farewell.

'Oh, yes. I know,' she said.

Back in her room at the Roebuck, Miss Teatime lit a cheroot and took her first whisky sip of the day. As she stared thoughtfully at the gulls swooping down past the blind eyes of the old warehouse, her fingers tapped the sheet of writing paper spread ready on the table before her. She was devising a simple insurance policy.

She picked up her pen.

My dear Inspector Purbright: The enclosed letters unexpectedly came to hand today. They were written by my friend, who calls himself Commander John Trelawney. You will see that I was mistaken about the handwriting. I can plead only that loyalty clouded my judgment. His address is not known to me at the moment, but I have no doubt that Mrs Staunch will be able to give you the information you need. As you will notice, the reference number is 4122.

Yours sincerely,
Lucilla Teatime.

She folded the note, pinned it to the three sheets of the commander's correspondence and put them all into an envelope. This she sealed and addressed.

Downstairs, she found the manager supervising the changing of flowers in the residents' lounge. He bustled up to her in immediate response to a smile of inquiry.

'I wish you to undertake a delicate but important commission, Mr Maddox.'

At once he was fussily intrigued.

She handed him the envelope.

'I am going out today and probably shall not be in for lunch,' she explained softly. 'I may even be away until early evening. If, however, I have not returned by eight o'clock, I want you to have this letter delivered straight away by hand.'

Maddox looked at the address and nodded earnestly. 'Eight o'clock,' he repeated.

'I am sure I can rely upon you, Mr Maddox.'

'You most certainly can.' He peered at her, suddenly anxious. 'I hope there's nothing, ah. . . .'

'Purely precautionary,' said Miss Teatime. 'As I believe you know, I am being well looked after.'

At the door she gave him a reassuring wave. Mr Maddox stared after her, his hand feeling for the edge of the envelope in his pocket.

The journey to Benstone, this time without incidental vigils at railway stations, was much more quickly accomplished than she had expected. It was not yet twelve when she halted the Renault just short of the series of lane turnings where she had lost Trelawney's car two nights before.

She took out the map. Three buildings were marked at distances from the road that could reasonably be supposed to be within earshot. There was one along each lane.

She started off again and took the left turn. About fifty yards from the road, a big, sombre farmhouse loomed behind an overgrown hedge. Miss Teatime did not need to get out of the car to see that no one had occupied it for many years. Through one of the glassless windows she caught a brief glimpse of sky as she drove by; part of the roof at the back had collapsed.

After returning to the main road, she made her way up the second lane – that on the right. She saw first a chimney stack and then thatch appear in a cleft in the lane's banking.

Soon she drew level with a broad gateway. Beyond it was a gravelled enclosure in front of a long, low, white-walled cottage.

A garage large enough for two cars had been built against the right hand gable and painted white. It was open and empty.

Miss Teatime drove into the enclosure, made a half-circle turn, and got out of the car. She knocked on the front door of the cottage. After a minute, she knocked again, more insistently. There was no response. The door was locked.

She explored, going from window to window.

The interior had every sign of expensive conversion. There was central heating and a wealth of good, modern furniture. The kitchen was generously, almost lavishly, equipped.

It was not until she looked into the glass-paned annexe at the back of the cottage, however, that she found a clue of the kind she was seeking.

Thrown across a bench was the suede leather driving jacket with fur collar and curiously pink-tinged octagonal buttons that Trelawney had been wearing when he took her to the Riverside Rest.

So far, so good.

Sensibly interpreting the empty feeling induced by the sight of the jacket as an indication that she needed lunch, Miss Teatime got into the car once more and drove the rest of the way into Chalmsbury.

She had a meal at an inn called – irresistibly, she thought – the Nelson and Emma, wandered for half an hour around the shops in St Luke's Square, and sat long enough on a bench outside the General Post Office to savour fully the grotesquerie of the town's war memorial opposite.

Then she returned to Low Benstone.

The cottage was still empty.

She sat in the car and smoked a cheroot.

A full hour went by.

Miss Teatime jerked upright in her seat, realizing that she had been about to doze off. She started the engine. A drive around the byways would be as pleasant a means as any of killing time.

But when she came back at nearly five o'clock, she saw that the big garage remained gaping, unoccupied.

She sat watching a trio of blackbirds chasing one another in and out of the hedge bottom near the gateway. They were angry and coquettish in turns. Every now and then, one would hop away from the others, stick tail and chest up in the air and stare at her officiously. She thought of that policeman waiting at the back of the Roebuck Hotel. Then, possibly by some chain of subconscious association, of window cleaners going up and down ladders in threes. Her eyes closed and the blackbirds were white, dive-bombing a bucket of blood.... They strolled towards her in naval uniform, saluting in the most supercilious manner imaginable....

Miss Teatime fell more and more deeply asleep.

Sergeant Love put down the phone and wearily struck out the last name left on his list of estate agents, valuers and auctioneers in Chalmsbury, Flaxborough and district. All he had gained from his labours was a sore throat and the suspicion that somewhere along the line he had made an unwise joke to a freemason friend of the chief constable.

He went in to Purbright and reported that if Brookside Cottage were indeed for sale, no one in the property trade was aware of it.

'No, well we had to check,' said Purbright. He made it sound easy, trivial almost.

'Would you like me to walk out to Benstone and ask at the cottage?' Love inquired bitterly.

Purbright glanced at the clock.

'Oh, not now, Sid. Leave it till morning.'

He went on with what he had been doing, but looked up again as Love noisily opened the door.

'I tell you what you *can* do. Give the county boys a ring at Chalmsbury and see if old Larch is in a good enough mood to get you the name of the occupants. It'll save you asking at the door when you go. You'd better say it's for me.'

Love knew that he better had. Chief Inspector Larch was a fearsome misanthrope and disciplinarian who, while conscientious within those rules he could not ignore, would have regarded a request from a mere sergeant as impertinence.

Even the quoting of Purbright's name produced nothing more helpful from Hector Larch than an impatient grunt and a half promise to see what he could do if ever he disposed of a mountain of much more important matters.

In fact, Larch obtained the information in less than five minutes, simply by demanding it of the front office clerk whom he knew to live at Benstone. But he saved it for a couple of hours more on principle.

Thus it was that Purbright was anxiously examining the contents of an envelope that had just been delivered to his home by a porter from the Roebuck Hotel when there came a ring on the extension line from the police station.

By the time he replaced the receiver, he was looking more anxious still.

Chapter Eighteen

MISS TEATIME SWAM UP OUT OF SLEEP WITH THE sense of a cold current dragging at her legs. Then it seemed to be a wind. She shivered and opened her eyes. The car door was open.

'Ahoy, there! Why don't you come ashore?'

The big fleshy face, converging roundly to its prow-like nose, hung just below the car roof. Trelawney's eyes peered down with a glint of calculating amusement. His broad, stooped shoulders shadowed her.

'Good evening,' said Miss Teatime steadily. She knew by the greyness of the light that she had slept for at least a couple of hours.

He stepped back and remained holding open the door.

Miss Teatime got out of the car.

He nodded towards the cottage. 'So you found my little surprise all by yourself,' he said, then added, more harshly: 'As I did yours.'

'I think we had better go inside, Mr Trelawney.'

He lingered a moment, his smile thin and fixed, then he turned and walked to the front door of the cottage.

They entered a long, low-beamed room, thickly carpeted in blue, with yellow cushioned light wood furniture, an enormous television set and, in the three deep window recesses, earthenware bowls of cactus and succulents. The walls were of pale grey rough cast plaster. On that facing the windows hung a Gauguin reproduction, its flowers and flesh glowing like a stove.

Miss Teatime sat primly on a chair near the centre of the room, her handbag on her knee.

Trelawney walked slowly to one of the windows, where he remained with his back towards her.

'As a preliminary to our discussion. . . .' she began.

He spun round. 'Oh, it's to be a discussion, is it? How nice. Will you begin, or shall I?'

'Please do not be childish. I was saying that as a preliminary I should like to ask you not to use any more of those jolly jack tar expressions. I have suffered a number of courtships in my life, but never before one which made me seasick.'

'You'll have something worse than seasickness to worry about before I've finished with you, woman.' He had flushed, and yet he spoke quite calmly and deliberately.

'Threats will serve the interest of neither of us,' Miss Teatime replied. 'They are ill mannered and unbusinesslike.'

'I suppose that as a professional swindler you are all for the smooth approach?'

Miss Teatime sighed. 'There you go again, Mr Trelawney. Abuse will get us nowhere.'

'So you don't deny being a swindler, then?'

'That is not what is worrying you. It was the word "professional" on which you laid stress, I noticed. If the acquisition of smoothness will allay your jealousy and bad temper, do for goodness' sake stop imagining that amateurism is a virtue.'

He leaned back against the wall and folded his hands. High in one cheek a nerve throbbed spasmodically.

'What did you come here for?'

'For compensation, Mr Trelawney. I do not consider that I have been fairly treated.'

'*You* don't cons. . . .'

She raised a hand. 'No, please let me finish. Your intention was to acquire a valuable motor boat by handing to a distressed family what you knew to be a worthless cheque. It was a very shabby design, which was thwarted thanks only to my having invented both the boat and the family's distress.

'Thus your gain was an easy conscience, and it was I who accomplished it.

'But what did I receive in return?

'No one can compute the worth of an easy conscience; it is a priceless commodity. And so when I decided to draw a fee that would little more than cover my expenses, it hurt rather than embarrassed me to find that you had lied about putting five hundred pounds at my disposal.

'For that hurt, I believe I am fully entitled to recompense, and if you will now be good enough to write me a cheque – a genuine cheque this time – for five hunred pounds, I shall be much obliged, Mr Trelawney.'

Miss Teatime drew herself a little more erect in her chair, smoothed her skirt and stared solemnly out of the window.

Trelawney said nothing for several seconds. He was grinning as he explored one nostril with the tip of his middle finger. When he had finished, he looked at the finger and wiped it on the wall behind his back.

He walked across and sat in a chair facing her, three feet away. He leaned forward and nodded.

'All right. Joke over. Now just what is it you think you're up to?'

She turned to him and raised her eyebrows. 'This is not a joke, Mr Trelawney. I have told you quite simply what I require.'

'Do you mean to say,' he said slowly and with no trace now of amusement, 'that you have the bloody neck to come out here and try and drag money out of me after what's happened?'

'I do,' said Miss Teatime.

'You know what you are, don't you? You're a prissy-mouthed, four-eyed, chiselling bitch, and you can go to hell!'

She looked at him appraisingly.

'If you really feel that we have arrived at the exchange of compliments stage, I can only assure you that the choice between an hour of your company, Mr Trelawney, and being sewn for a week in a sack of discarded boil dressings would be by no means easy to make.'

'Cow!'

She shrugged and looked at her watch.

'I advise you not to waste further time on thinking up expletives. You lack the talent. If you will write me out that cheque at once, a great deal of trouble will be avoided – for you in particular.'

Watching her all the time, he moved his chair a little closer. There was menace now in his quietness, in the slow, deliberate manner of his watching and listening. With the tip of his tongue he felt his upper lip.

'Go on,' he said. 'This trouble. . . . Tell me.'

'The situation,' said Miss Teatime, 'is not without a certain piquancy. I shall come to that aspect in a moment. First, though, let us acknowledge a few facts of which you imagine I am unaware.

'I have known for some little time that your intentions towards me are strictly dishonourable. You are doubtless vain enough to have supposed that I would not guess, but it really was not very difficult.

'I also happen to know – although I claim no personal credit for this – that you have already successfully imposed on the credulity of at least two other women. I know their names. One was called Reckitt, the other Bannister. And I know that the police are looking for the man who enginered their disappearance. For you, in fact.'

Trelawney, crouched on the edge of his chair as if in readiness to spring, was staring straight into her eyes. She looked back calmly.

'Now here is the amusing thing,' she went on. 'Or at least I hope you will see the humour of it because then you might stop glaring quite so unpleasantly. The only reason why you have not been arrested is that I have personally vouched for your integrity. There, now – what do you think of that?'

'What the hell do you mean?'

'Oh, dear, you are so curmudgeonly. . . .'

'What did you tell them?'

'That you are a bluff and honest sea-dog, of course. A

sincere suitor. A gentleman whose handwriting bears not the faintest resemblance to that of the villain whose letters to poor Mrs Bannister have been discovered by the police.'

After a long silence, Trelawney's hunched frame relaxed. He leaned back into his chair.

'In other words, you thought you'd set up a nice little line in blackmail.'

'Your moral judgments are as odious as your maritime metaphors. Kindly keep both to yourself.'

'I don't believe this nonsense about letters.'

Unhurriedly, Miss Teatime opened her bag. She handed the photograph to Trelawney without comment.

He looked at it, then raised his eyes. 'You say you've told them this isn't my writing?'

'Emphatically.'

'And that Commander Jack Trelawney's a fine chap who wouldn't hurt a fly?'

'By a great effort of will, yes.'

'So I am not suspected of the awful crimes the police imagine have been committed?'

'No.'

He smiled. It was like a crack running across ice.

'Oh, dear,' sighed Miss Teatime, 'you are so woefully transparent, Jackie boy.'

'Am I?'

'You are saying to yourself: Knock this lady off as well and all will be hunky-dory.'

'It does seem a damn good idea. In fact, I'm sold on it.'

She shook her head. 'No, I do not think you are, really. Already there has crept into that incommodious mind the realization that I should never have been fool enough to come here without taking some precaution.'

'Oh, and what precaution?'

'It is in the form of a time limit. If I am not back at my hotel by eight o'clock, the police at Flaxborough will receive a packet containing your letters.'

'And my name and address, no doubt,' added Trelawney carelessly.

'No – just the means of learning them with singularly little trouble.'

'How little?'

'Simply a peep into the files of that excellent matrimonial bureau, Jack dear. Or should I say Mr Four-one-double-two?'

For a moment, he looked genuinely puzzled. Then he smiled, grinned, began to laugh aloud.

Miss Teatime heard a door close behind her. She looked round quickly.

'But surely you didn't imagine that my husband's name would be on the files, Miss Teatime? There isn't a four-one-double-two. I think a burglar must have lifted it.'

Donald Staunch rose and grasped his wife's arm.

'The car,' he said. 'Get it out of sight somewhere and come straight back. I'll want you to stay with her while I ... see to things.'

Inspector Purbright found Love at his lodgings, being dotingly administered a late high tea by his landlady, Mrs Cusson.

He plucked him from the scarcely begun feast of buttered haddock, wholemeal scones, tinned oranges, Carnation milk and Eccles cakes; bustled him past a tearfully protesting Mrs Cusson, enemy of malnutrition; and thrust him to the car.

'You drive, Sid. Hunger's good for alertness.'

It seemed a pretty good propellant as well. They were passing through Benstone Ferry less than twenty minutes later.

'Up here and across the common,' Purbright directed.

Four minutes more.

'First turning off on the right, now. Mind, it's sharp.'

The car crunched to a stop on the gravel before Brookside Cottage. Purbright reached the door first. He knocked sharply and repeatedly on the thick wood.

Pausing, he heard movement within the house. The sergeant was beside him now.

'They're in,' said Purbright. Again he knocked. They heard footsteps inside. The steps receded. Purbright knocked even harder.

'Sid, you'd better go round to.... No, wait a bit.' The footsteps were coming back. The door opened.

'Good evening, Mrs Staunch.' Without further preliminary, the inspector stepped past her, followed immediately by Love.

Sylvia Staunch turned from the door and stared at them furiously.

'Would you kindly explain what this is all about.'

'Where is Miss Teatime?'

'Miss *Who*?' A perplexed glare.

'Your client. Miss Teatime. I have reason to believe she came here to see your husband.'

'Why on earth should she want to see my husband? He has nothing whatever to....'

'Is he in, Mrs Staunch?'

'Not at the moment, no.'

Love looked at the inspector. 'Both cars are in the garage, sir.'

'Well, Mrs Staunch?'

'I think he's gone to post a letter.'

Her composure was being re-established, her bewilderment more artistically controlled.

'But I am not going to stand here and have questions fired at me without knowing the reason for them. What authority have you got to come trampling in here, anyway?'

'We suspect felony, Mrs Staunch. That may be a somewhat stuffy answer, but it will serve at least until your husband returns.' He drew a curtain aside and peered out. 'Which I trust will not be long. How far away is the post box?'

'At the end of the lane.'

'Odd that we did not see him.'

'There's a path from the back. It's quicker.'

Purbright nodded. He motioned Mrs Staunch to sit down.

'I might as well tell you now,' he said to her, 'that we shall probably ask your husband to return to Flaxborough with us.'

'But what an earth for?'

'We think he may be able to help us to get at the truth about one or two matters.'

'You don't have to use jargon with me, inspector. That just means you think he's done something. What, though? Why can't you say? And for God's sake what's all this about that Teatime woman?'

'If, as you say, she has not been here, you have no need to worry on her account, Mrs Staunch.'

'Yes, but why did. . . .'

Purbright had held up his hand. He was listening intently.

From the back of the house came a small scuffling, fumbling sound. They heard a door being opened.

Mrs Staunch jumped up from her chair, but at once Purbright caught and held her arm.

The back door clicked shut. Someone was walking across the tiled floor of the kitchen.

'Don!' Mrs Staunch shouted. 'There are two policemen who are asking a lot of silly questions. We are in here. I wish you would come and tell them that they're. . . .'

The door from the kitchen was pushed open. There entered a slightly dishevelled, slightly unsteady Miss Teatime.

Mrs Staunch stared, her mouth slowly opening. Then from the mouth came a scream.

'Where's Don? Where's my husband? Damn you! Where's Don?'

She tried to throw herself forward, but Purbright's grip did not yield.

Miss Teatime gazed at her regretfully.

'I am afraid he is in that cesspool thing down the garden.'

Mrs Staunch's screams subsided into a low, sobbing howl. Her body folded helplessly across the inspector's arm.

'I really am very sorry,' said Miss Teatime. 'But it was his idea entirely to go waltzing about in the dark with his arms round my waist. The cover was off, you know.'

She turned her sorrowful gaze to Sergeant Love and added, as if for his own special information:

'I bloody nearly fell in myself.'